MISTER BONES &
the
SCRIMSHANDER

THE CHESS CLUB

IN PAST HISTORY ✳

Chess has been with us almost beyond measured time. Written records of the game come to light from Persia around the mid fourth, or fifth century. To own a chess set was highly un-usual, as each individual piece had to be hand carved. No two were alike, and each chess set differed in several ways. And yes, some would have been very rudimentary in design. Those few who made these chess sets had to understand the game to know what a finished chess piece would look like, and to represent.

Chess sets were so valuable that they were often left as part of an estate upon one's death. To commission a chess set to be made for an individual would require a wealthy patron and the length of time for the person doing the carving to acquire the chosen materials. This could be any material that offered an ability to be carved. Many substances were tried, even rock crystal. but the more common were that of hard woods, and Ivory. The Ivory may have been from an elephant's tusk, or that of a walrus tooth. In time even metal was used, such as silver, or gold, but these were most likely cast, and finished with fine tools then polished.

To place a value on a chess set for sale in a market place would be a rarity, and would have been a gamble as it would have been whatever the seller could obtain from the buyer. The better the workmanship, the higher the cost.

This story is about a seaman who spent his time at sea carving chess pieces. Word would have spread about the entire area of someone who had the ability to produce fine chess pieces and they would have been sought out by the wealthy or those who were influential.

NOTE:
One thing to remember about the game of chess. It's like a whirlpool. The danger is in the center.
The chess Queen, lovely as she is, a seemingly quiet individual, gentle to those whom she favors, is in reality someone who loves a good battle.

At the end of this book you will find a brief history of the characters used in this story.

One last note. The language used in this story line does not adhere to that of the time frame used in the story. To do so would befuddle most readers of today.

ONE
CHESS SET ✭

Captain Neuman and Richard Humphry, owner of the shipping company whose ships and the one the captain was currently in command of, is the 'John T. Franklin', The two men were just finishing going over the details for the upcoming voyage to the spice Islands that the captain was about to embark upon. The captain was to seek various spices for the markets, such as Pepper, Cloves, Cinnamon, Mace, Nutmeg, even Wine if cargo space permitted and good wines could be found. Finished with the cargo listing, and as the captain rose from the chair near Richard's desk he motioned the fine chess set he had seen on a side table nearby. "That's a fine chess set Richard."

"Aye, yes it is. It was carved by a master carver."

"I'm not one to play the game, but this set looks a bit different from those I've seen before."

"Yes, well it is of the finest of light and dark Ivory. The chess board is made of Ebony and white Mahogany. The table stand base that supports it is of Rosewood."

"Richard, If I understand it correctly, chess sets can become quite expensive?"

"That they are, and because of the time it takes for a craftsman to make each piece, individually it may take a great deal of time to finish a chess set.. This set took three years to finish. Still, the sum of eighty six pounds seems well spent."

The captain stopped in his tracks, looked at the chess set once again and replied. "Mother of God. That's a Kings ransom."

"Yes, but you see it would have been one hundred pounds, if I was not in position to obtain the exotic woods for the craftsman, Mister Bowman. It is he who provides these magnificent chess sets you see here before you. Thus, I'm able to get a reduced price. A trade off, you might say. And, I've another offer I may put to him in the future."

TWO
SPICE ISLANDS ✶
It was late May 1829 and the good ship John T. Franklin was lying along side the wharf in Hull harbour as she was laying aboard the last of her needs. Which, among the ship's supplies for repairs and other items in common use, largely this consisted of salt horse, heavily salted beef, greasy pork, beans, rice, or potatoes, hard biscuits, and molasses. The intention of the ship's, captain, and the cook, would be to obtain, at ports of call, fresh water, fruits, and vegetables were to be taken aboard to supplement what was now placed aboard as well. At sea they would take advantage of sea turtles, dolphins, sea birds, as well as fish. The ships carpenter, the blacksmith and Sailmaker, always tried to keep their supply of stores well supplied.

This day the Captain and first mate were to be found waiting at the inboard end of the gangplank as the remaining crew came aboard. As Samuel stepped off the gangplank and onto the ships main deck, the ship's Captain greeted him. "Bones, You've been aboard for a few days now is your gear stowed?"

"Aye, sir. Just ashore for to get a few new knives, sir."

"It's good to have you aboard as Port Bosun."

"Aye, sir, and I thank you for taking me on sir." Then Samuel moved below to his cabin in steerage. A space he would share with another boatswain.

The first mate standing close by and learning each hands name as the last of them came aboard, and as a new mate to this Captain, he was well aware that many of the ship's crew had shipped with this captain before, and he said. "Bones, ats an odd name, Captain."

"Aye but that's not his given name, just what the hands call him. He carves Ivory in his own time. Chess pieces I think they are? The Starboard Bosun is another like him. He carves scrimshaw."

As Samuel was walking away to go below, the first mate said. "He speaks a bit like that of a gentleman sir."

"He's had some schooling I think before his family passed on from the sickness while he was young. His father was a man of some means, but left nothing for the lad. Mister Humphry signed him on as ship crew many years ago. He's worked hard and been moved up to Bosun nine years ago now."

After the last of the crew was aboard, the crews girl friends or wives having departed the wharf as well as the Captain's wife, he turned to the mate along side and said. "Have Mister Rollins get us underway on the morning ebb tide. He's to have the Starboard watch."

"Aye sir."

Upon returning to his cabin Captain Neuman found young John, the boy apprenticed to him as cabin boy, storing the rest of his gear away in his sea chest. His berth was set in the forward Starboard corner of the captain's cabin. John understood that his role aboard as cabin boy. was that of the captain's messenger. And, as he was to learn later, many other chores were to be his as well. What he didn't know was how much responsibility had been placed on the captain for his well being and his education about running a ships and her crews.

"John, lad."

John stopped what he was doing and looked at the captain, "Sir?"

"John you should go forward to the Fo'c'sle and learn each man's name and where he bunks. You'll need to know this so in the dark of night, or in stormy seas you can find each of them and wake them for their watch if need be. You will also need to learn where the mates and the Bosun's sleep and their names as well."

"Aye. Sir."

After John had left the cabin, the captain was thinking. *"I'll have my hands full with that lad. And, I'll have to address his well being to the crew."* As one of two his ship's clock chimed six times, he went to his work table and began writing the day's events into the ship's log book.

The ship's clocks were new ones given to him, and required daily attention. One was set for the time aboard the ship during her daily travels, the other was set for the time in their home port. He, and the ship's crew would retire early this night as the coming morning would bring activity that was to last for many months to come.

THREE
UNDER WAY ✶

In the dark morning hours John had found the mates bunks in the Port gun cabin, and had waken them. The first mate, Mister Mirelles, instructed John to wake both of the Bosuns, so as to make the ship ready for sea. John had gone to the Boatswains quarters that was found amidship in steerage. He had to be careful with his footing because the Bosun's quarters were odd shaped and their gear was grouped in two different areas according to their needs. John had already seen many odd tools in boxes on the deck around a sturdy Bosun's table fastened to the aft bulkhead when he'd been here the day before and learning their whereabouts. These had made him curious and he would ask later what they were for.

After rising, both of the Bosun's went forward with John just after seven bells rang on the ship's bell found near the ship's helm. They were waking all foremast hands. In the forecastle the Bosun's followed the bunks that lined the hull of the narrow triangular shaped room under the ship's bow deck. There was a lot of grumbling and cursing, but they all began turning out.

At eight bells, 0400 hours, the captain joined the first and second mates on the quarterdeck with the boatswains on the main deck below. The helmsman, Jeffery, from the Starboard watch, stood at the helm ready to take the ship to sea on the first mates orders.

The captain spoke to the first mate. "Mister Mirelles I see we have a favorable wind this morning."

The first mate looked aloft at the mastheads seeing the wind pennants direction. "Aye, sir. We won't be needing the ship's boats to take us off the wharf, Sir."

"Very well, loose the ship Mister Mirelles."

"Aye, Sir." He turned to face the Bosuns waiting below on the main deck just forward of the mizzen mast. "Mister Rollins you have the watch, hoist your jibs, and when we are free of the wharf Mister Bowman, set the Spanker gaft aloft."

Both Bosuns replied "Aye, aye sir." Shouts could be heard from both men as they gave orders to the crew to do as the first mate ordered. Shortly the two jibs were hauled up the forestays and belayed. The Port watch hands were handling the ships mooring lines as they were taken aboard and stowed in their normal places while at sea. When the bow, which was falling off the wharf with the breeze, the Spanker was hauled up the aft side of the mizzen mast and belayed until a final setting was made while underway. She slowly made her way toward the open sea.

At 0500, two bells had sounded from the quarterdeck and the first mate ordered the mainsails and mizzen to be set. Hands from the Starboard watch, were on the yards to free the canvas and as the sails filled with the offshore breeze, they were hauled to the best angle that would fill them with the Port winds and place the ship on a down wind reach. The Port watch had been sent below to rest for their upcoming watch which would take place at eight bells. Now less than four hours distant. The watches at sea were set to be four hours on watch, four hours off watch. Unless all hands were needed topside, then anything could take place in the otherwise normal watch routine.

Satisfied all was well the Captain said to his first mate. "You have the deck Mister Mirelles. I'll be below."

"Aye, Sir"

John, who had been fascinated while watching the ship being taken to sea, simply followed the captain below. In the captains cabin the Captain said. "John you might want to catch some sleep lad. When at sea you will want to get your rest when you can."

John had no sooner laid down on his cot when he was fast asleep. The captain was working on the ship's log noting the morning's activities for getting underway.

On this day of the Lord, we have put to sea. The Starboard watch is set. Our destination is to the Spice Islands. There we are to take a cargo aboard for the ship's company, Humphry Limited. The ship seems well as are all hands.

Captain, James Neuman

When the ships clock chimed eight bells, John was given the task of taking a fresh Sand glass to the helmsman on watch. He was to do this each morning for the entire passage. This was to start the day with a sand glass that had not been warmed so the sand would flow more freely, thus shortening the watch for the crew during the night. A ploy that had been discovered by the ships mates in the past.

On the third day at sea John was at the captain's side as he took the noon sun sighting to fix the ships position on the charts used for maintaining a record of their passage over the seas. As he stood there he had looked down at the main deck and saw Samuel sitting on the deck leaning his back against the cook shack bulkhead. As the captain finished his notes, john asked. "What's Mister Bones doing, Sir"

The captain glanced briefly down to have a look, then replied. "I believe he is carving an ivory chess piece."

"Can I go ask him, Sir?"

"I see no harm in that, Lad."

John stood quietly waiting nearby, and when Samuel looked his way, John asked. "The captain tells me you are carving a chess piece?"

"Aye, that I am." It was quiet for a few moments between them, then Samuel asked. "Do you play the game of chess lad?"

" I've not learned of the game, Mister Bones, Sir. But I've heard tell it's a royal game."

Samuel considered his next question carefully, and decided it would be okay to inquire. "It's known as a royal game, but anyone can play the game, You don't have to be part of the King's court to play chess. Now that you know that, would you like to learn the game? I could teach you while we are at sea if you like."

John's mind took but a few seconds to make up is decision. "Aye, sir. I would like that indeed sir." This would be a new thing to learn and take up some of his time and the days at sea.

"If you don't have duties to attend to now, why don't you sit along side me and we'll start with how the game is played and some of how it came about as well."

They spoke for some time, and by the time they were finishing their conversation they were on a first name basis. It was unusual for John to call someone outside of his own family, by their given name. "John, on the morrow you and I will go see Mister Chips. We'll have him make some simple wood pieces that you can use as chessmen while you learn the game. And we'll speak with Needles, the sailmaker. I'll have him make you a chess board of sailcloth so you can roll it up to keep in your sea chest.

FOUR
JOHN ✮

The following afternoon, with the hastily assembled chess set, Samuel took John below to his quarters. The chess board was of sailcloth with squares marked off with charcoal lines, as well as the needed colored squares, then sealed with whale oil to lock in the colors and to waterproof it as well. The pieces of wood to be used, were placed upon the table he and Timothy Rollins used for their carving needs. While John watched, Samuel produced a ink quill and a small bottle of black ink. Then he began printing a single letter on the top of each piece of wood. And an inked line was marked around the center of the black chess pieces so they could be seen more easily.

John asked. "Why do you place a 'N' on top of the piece you said we were going to use as Knights?"

Samuel was surprised and asked. "You know your letters, John?"

"Aye, My mum showed me my letters and my numbers as well."

Smiling with the thought of this young fellow and his Knowledge of things, he continued. "Well the King will get the 'K' on its top. So the 'N' will tell yo which piece is the Knight. Do you Understand?"

"I think so. It tells me we don't have three Kings in the game."

John's lessons had started taking place topside that same day. During their conversation Samuel learned the name of John's patron and that of his secretary, Martin. He had dealings with both in the recent past. He also became aware that John was very good with numbers.

FIVE
LESSONS ✳

It was at the end of the Port watch when the second mate
came to Samuel. "Bones, Captain Neuman sent me to fetch
you."

Samuel worried as he followed the mate aft to the captains'
quarters. He couldn't remember doing something that was
against the ship's articles. The mate knocked at the door to
the captains' cabin, and when he heard. "Come." He opened
the door and stepped inside. Samuel was close behind.

The captain rose from his chart table and said. "That'll be all
Mister Mason." The second mate hesitated as he wanted to
know what the captain had wanted with the Bosun, but he left
the cabin. As the captain and the Bosun were the only people
in the cabin the mate waited outside the door hoping to hear
part of the words being spoken, but could make no sense of
them so he returned topside.

"Mister Bowman, join me here at my chart table."

Samuel sat in one of the two chairs arranged at the table and
he saw young John's chess set in the center of the table.. The
captain said. "I've watched young John look at these things
here." His fingers pointing to the ill conceived chess set.
"John tells me you are teaching him the game of chess."

"Aye, sir. I didn't think it would cause a problem, Sir?"

15

"Oh, it is no problem Mister Bowman. No problem at all for John. It is I who have the problem. You see, I don't know how to advise him when he questions me about the game. You see, I don't know the game myself.

"I'm sorry to have fetched a worry for you, Captain."

The two of them sat quietly for just a few short seconds, then Captain Neuman said. "There is a way to help me with this problem."

"Sir?" Samuel would do whatever it took to allow him to keep teaching John the game. The lad seemed to have a way of learning quickly.

"You could teach me the game as well. But, . . . it would have to be known only to the three of us. If you get my meaning?"

"We can do that, Sir" He knew exactly what the captain was saying. The crew couldn't be allowed to think he was getting special treatment from the ship's captain.

"I'm curious Mister Bowman. John tells me you know your letters as well. How is that?"

Samuel felt odd having this kind of discussion with his ship's Captain, but started to answer the question with. "My mother taught me most things. My father did as well. But, they've passed. So now when I'm ashore I play chess at the 'Queen's Inn' And the gentlemen who come there, speak to me about the game as we play. So, I've learned more from them."

"You say, The gentlemen from Towne play chess there?"

"Aye, Sir. Quite a few of the Gentry come to the 'Queen's Inn,' Many times they place wagers as they play the game."

"You mean these are men of means. Those that live in fine houses and such?"

"Aye, sir."
It was at the end of the Port watch when the second mate came to Samuel. "Bones, Captain Neuman sent me to fetch you."

Samuel worried as he followed the mate aft to the captains' quarters. He couldn't remember doing something that was against the ship's articles. The mate knocked at the door to the captains' cabin, and when he heard. "Come." He opened the door and stepped inside. Samuel was close behind.

The captain rose from his chart table and said. "That'll be all Mister Mason." The second mate hesitated as he wanted to know what the captain had wanted with the Bosun, but he left the cabin. As the captain and the Bosun were the only people in the cabin the mate waited outside the door hoping to hear part of the words being spoken, but could make no sense of them so he returned topside.

"Mister Bowman, join me here at my chart table."

Samuel sat in one of the two chairs arranged at the table and he saw young John's chess set in the center of the table.. The captain said. "I've watched young John look at these things here." His fingers pointing to the ill conceived chess set. "John tells me you are teaching him the game of chess."

"Aye, sir. I didn't think it would cause a problem, Sir?"

"Oh, it is no problem Mister Bowman. No problem at all for John. It is I who have the problem. You see, I don't know how to advise him when he questions me about the game. You see, I don't know the game myself.

"I'm sorry to have fetched a worry for you, Captain."

The two of them sat quietly for just a few short seconds, then Captain Neuman said. "There is a way to help me with this problem."

"Sir?" Samuel would do whatever it took to allow him to keep teaching John the game. The lad seemed to have a way of learning quickly.

"You could teach me the game as well. But, . . . it would have to be known only to the three of us. If you get my meaning?"

"We can do that, Sir" He knew exactly what the captain was saying. The crew couldn't be allowed to think he was getting special treatment from the ship's captain.

"I'm curious Mister Bowman. John tells me you know your letters as well. How is that?"

Samuel felt odd having this kind of discussion with his ship's Captain, but started to answer the question with. "My mother taught me most things. My father did as well. But, they've passed. So now when I'm ashore I play chess at the 'Queen's Inn' And the gentlemen who come there, speak to me about the game as we play. So, I've learned more from them."

"You say, The gentlemen from Towne play chess there?"

"Aye, Sir. Quite a few of the Gentry come to the 'Queen's Inn,' Many times they place wagers as they play the game."

"You mean these are men of means. Those that live in fine houses and such?"

"Aye, sir."

SIX

CARGO ✶

Samuel carved his chess pieces during the daylight hours, but in the evenings, while not on watch, he would carefully make his way to the captains cabin where he would teach both, the captain and Young John how to play chess. It seemed as if the only person who knew of this arrangement, other than the three of them, as was Timothy, his bunk mate and fellow Bosun.

During the passage to the Island of Santa Cruz, where they would take on fresh stores, the captain and young John had done nicely in learning how the game was to be played. Samuel understood that now he had to make them understand that just knowing how the chess pieces moved, was not all there was to the game. It required much more understanding, and the mind had to think farther ahead.

It had taken the ship and crew into the dark hours of the twenty-seventh day to arrive at an anchorage just offshore of Santa Cruz where they would arrange for fresh vegetables and water. Also to come aboard were a few chickens for the captains and mates table. Now the next part of the journey would take them to the Spice Islands. Captain Neuman's estimate was that it would take them nearly seven weeks to make the crossing. Still, his ship, "John T. Franklin" was known as a good ship.

It was known ashore that Captain Neuman was a fair ships master, and that Mister Humphry who was the owner of the shipping company was generous to his ship's crews.

Only the best were signed aboard and their wages were above those paid by other shipping companies. This alone kept things aboard ship at a level of forgiveness not found aboard other ships. The times away from home were often lengthy but rewarding as well.

Two nights before the next sea passage was to start, and a quiet night in the anchorage when a small crew of three men stood watch, the Bosun's were not needed and allowed to remain in their quarters. Samuel and Timothy were using one of four ships lamp in their cabin. The Spermaceti oil they were using in their lamp was the best they could have , and they needed it for the best lighting while they were applying their artistic carving skills to the ongoing pieces they were trying to finish.

Timothy was drawing a mermaid onto the side of a large horn he'd found in a market before leaving their home port, when Samuel mentioned. "The captain told me that during following seas as the ship rose and fell, that the chess pieces they are using will slide off the edge of the captains chart table. That's where they play chess. I need to fix that somehow. Perhaps a raised edge around the edge of the board."

Timothy looked at his friend who was carving the last of the Pawns for his next Ivory chess set. He said. "Samuel, let me have a look at that one you are working on now."

As he was handed the pawn he turned it over to look at the bottom, then said. " I'm thinking you could bore a small hole in the bottom of these chess pieces, then put a short round plug in the hole. And then bore the same hole into the middle of the squares on your chess board so's to put the piece into the hole where you want it to go, and it will stay there until you pick it up and move it to its next place."

Samuel was surprised at how simple that seemed. "I'd have to have the wooden plugs and some way to make the holes."

Timothy smiled. "I have boring tools, and you could get the pegs from Chips. I'm sure he would have plenty of them in his work shop."

In one of his three sea chests Samuel had a wooden chess set and chess board he had carved while ashore and waiting for one of Mister Humphry's ships to put to sea. The chess pieces and the board needed only to have a finish applied to them, then he would sell it when next he was ashore at home. The next day he'd gone to the ship's Carpenter and explained, "Chips I'm in need of some small pegs."

"Are yee now? What size would that be?"

Samuel showed him the length of his little finger nail and showed this to Chips. "This would do fine." Chips looked through several small boxes he'd made for such things, and when he found what he was looking for, he asked.

"Might these do what it is you need?" What he had handed the Bosun was a hole plug he used in his wood working projects, such as the new Binnacle housing he was currently putting together. It had to be assembled using wood dowels and could not have metal nails. So as not to pull the compass card off its rightful path.

"Aye. Those will do just right, sir. And I thank you." When he returned to his quarters he put the pegs in a small box that was within easy reach of his work space on the table. Timothy had shown him how to use the boring tool, so for the next several days he took great care to bore the holes into the bottom of the wooden chess pieces, then into the center of each square of the chess board. Then he sparingly used just a dab of 'Hide glue' on the end of each peg, he pushed the pegs up into the bottom of each chess piece. Then he left them to set for the rest of the day.

It was on one of these warm days and when the ship was becalmed that young John stopped to see what he was doing. He smiled at the boy as he said. "I'm putting varnish on this chess board."

John saw the holes in the board and asked. "Why do you have holes in the center of each square?"

"Ahh, well John this is a traveling chess set."

"I don't understand, You mean it can go places?"

"Well, any chess set can go places, but this is one that the pieces will stay in place as you play the game. Such as on a rolling deck."

SEVEN

CHESS *

John and the captain were in their second game of chess. The lamp lighting the table flickered as it cast its shadows across the chart table. The shadow moving from one side of the table to the other as the ship moved in her element. On occasion the movement of the ship would cause a chess piece, or two, to slip on the chart table's top ever so slightly. Just enough to be frustrating. To the two of them After one such adjustment the captain said. "This is a bother young John." As he reached out to retrieve the errant wooden chess piece.

"Aye, sir." Then he remembered an earlier conversation with Sam. " We could use one of Mister Bowman's travel chess sets, sir."

The captain looked at John and asked. "What kind of chess set?"

"He's just finishing his work on a chess set where the chessmen will stay in place while you play the game. It would work for us now."

"I've little knowledge of such things, but I'll ask the Bosun about it soon."

EIGHT
TRAVEL CHESS ✫

When Samuel knocked at the captains cabin door at the end of his watch and shortly after eight bells, he found both the captain and young John waiting for him. Their ability at playing the game had advanced well beyond his expectations. He reasoned that it was partly because of young John's interest. The boy seemed a natural at the chess board and studied it as often as he could. So, of course this would entail the Captains help as well. John would be a chess player to be wary of in the future.

As the three of them sat around the chart table, the ship rose with a following sea and they had to replace two chess pieces that had slid away from them. Then the captain broke the silence and said. "John tells that you have finished a traveling chess set."

Without thinking about the question in any depth, Samuel simply responded with. "Aye Sir."

"Perhaps, if I dare suggest, might we use it this evening?"

Now Samuel was paying attention. He thought. *"It would not harm the chess set, and I would have an idea of its value."* "I can fetch it if you've a mind sir?"

"Please do Mister Bowman, please do."

It was just a few short minutes before Samuel had returned with the new chess set. The chess set that had been on the chart table had been removed, so he placed the two sail canvas bags on the captain's chart table. As the captain opened the bags he lifted out the chess board first. It had a shine that reflected the lamps light on the table, a richness of the woods used to make the squares was very apparent as well. Even the holes in the surface of the board were finished with a fine varnish. Next the chess pieces were removed from the sailcloth bag that held them. The wood for the dark pieces was of Rosewood. The white pieces were of bleached Teak. Samuel could tell the captain was impressed with what he was handling. He held each piece gently, placing them in their proper places on the chess board and checking how they fit. Each just loose enough to make it easy to remove them and move them to another square.. Even young John was quiet as a game began between himself and the captain.

It had grown late and John had long gone to bed to sleep. Samuel was now explaining a middle game tactic to the captain, when the captain spoke up. When it happened that no one was around to hear them speak the captain called him by his given name. "Samuel what amount of funds would it take to make this chess set my own?"

"Captain. I mean no disrespect, sir, but my chess sets are often out of reach for most men. I think you might find it on the edge of yours, Still I've a good many hours carving this chess set and had intended to sell it to a fancy man at. ' The

Queen's Inn,"

"You're a man of rare talents' Samuel, still I'll pay whatever value you place upon this work of beauty." Samuel had placed a value on the set, but decided to test the captain. "Sir, the cost would be twenty five pounds sir."

The captain quietly sucked in his breath as he sat back in his chair, the price was higher than he felt it might be, but he had made the offer and it was indeed a very fine chess set, and would be highly approved by those men he dealt with at home. "I don't have the funds for you at the moment, but can fulfill my obligation to you when we are home again. Is that suitable Samuel?"

"Yes captain. You can pay the funds to Mister Humphry, he will put it in his steel box for my use as I need it sir," The captain was surprised at that request. "Mister Humphry keeps money for you in his strong box?"

"Aye, Sir. You see captain, this may be my last voyage. I'm to become a shopkeeper when we return home.'

The captain knew this to be a rare event, especially for a seaman. A man who spent his life on ships. Still, he said. " A shop keeper you say?"

"Aye, sir. I'm going to have a shop near "The Queen's Inn" Where I will carve and sell chess sets.".

NINE
TIMOTHY ✷

Later as Samuel thought about the talk with the captain, and his future wishes, He began to think about other things having to do with bringing customers into his shop. And, as he was thinking about this, his eyes alighted on some of Timothy's artistic ability in the form of a scrimshaw Mermaid being carved upon a horn on his side of the work table that they shared.

An idea occurred to him so he went to find Timothy. He found him standing next to his favored helmsman, Jeffery. "Mister Rollins, a word if you will."

Timothy looked quickly at the binnacle, noting the compass course, and said to the helmsman . "You might want to fall of just a bit so's your topsail fills properly. You've wavered a bit."

Then he turned to face Samuel, and nodded his head in agreement. And the two men moved to the downwind side of the quarterdeck. Samuel began a lengthy explanation about what his intentions were once they were back ashore. How he had the funds for a shop, and where it was to be found. Then he ventured a question. "So, Tim, would you have an interest in joining me in this venture."

Timothy was struck by the enormity of the offer. Never in his imagination had he ever considered such a thing in his life. His mind raced with the thought. *'A shopkeeper, good lord how wonderful that would be.'* He was quiet so long that Samuel worried he had made an error in the invitation to join him. Then suddenly, Timothy replied. "Sam I would be in your debt eternally for such a chance to join you in this shop of yours." A hand shake was all it took to seal the agreement.

TEN
ARRIVAL ✶

The passage to Bridgetown in the West Indies had taken them much longer than expected. The weather had been exceptional and in their favor. But the winds had been light as well. It was just a few days short of three months when late in the day the man at the masthead lookout called down. "Land ho, two points off the Port bow."

Within minutes the captain had been summoned and he and his officers were gathered on the quarterdeck. The captain was letting the men present take turns using his spyglass to scan the horizon for the Island ahead. He himself had already taken a good look. Benjamin, the helmsman Samuel favored most, was at the helm as the captain gave an order for their approach to the anchorage.

"Mister Mason."

The second mate answered. "Sir?"

"We'll stand offshore until first light in the morning."

"Aye, Sir. I'll make ready the anchor and for its being put on the bottom as you wish when we are in the place of your choice on the morrow, Sir"

"You should also lower and furl your main and mizzen canvas. Perhaps go in close under a Spanker and jibs. That will give us some control of her wanderings, but we have the time to do so."

"Aye, sir."

Late the following morning found the 'John T. Franklin' anchored in ten fathoms off the beach at Bridgetown. The Port watch crew had the watch and Samuel, as was the first mate, taking sights on prominent locations onshore so as to maintain a vigil on the ships' location. They wanted to be sure she did not drag her anchor if the wind came up. The captains skiff had been lowered over the side awaiting his need to go ashore and to make ready to take on fresh water and vegetables. He would also have to contact someone from the Islands authorities to make arrangements to purchase the spices that Mister Humphry had asked him to acquire.

ELEVEN
HOMEWARD BOUND ✶
With the Captain ashore, Mister Mirelles took command of the ships loading and storing the bundles and boxes of spices and tea that came aboard. Mister Mason was ashore directing the loading of the ship's longboats and those of the porters who were supplying the things the captain was himself purchasing. The Tea merchants had their own longboats to deliver goods to waiting ships and Mister Mason took advantage of any space on their boats to deliver other goods to the ship as well.

At the end of day six, captain Neuman and the mates were assembled on the quarterdeck watching the last of the supplies being stowed in the ships hold. It had gone well, and he was pleased with the efficiency of the crew. He was saying. "Mister Mirelles, and Mister Mason, you two did six fine days work getting our cargo loaded and stowed below. I'll see to it that you receive a reward for your efforts."

Both men smiled and thanked him. They also acknowledged the fact that the crew was well organized, due to the Bosuns. Captain Neuman agreed and hoped he could give them something for their efforts at the end of the voyage, other than just verbal praise.

To end the conversations, the captain said. "Set the watch for taking our anchor aboard at first morning light. We are ready to head home."

The mates called the crew to the aft main deck and gave instructions for Mister Rollins to make ready the Starboard watch to take the ship to sea in the morning. All hands were to be on deck as needed, then normal watches would begin.

Captain Neuman was b ring his ships log up to date as he listed their cargo below. In part it read.

This day, we finished loading and storing our cargo aboard. The ship's crew worked tirelessly and I wish to see that they are rewarded as can be arranged with Mister Humphry. We have, Over one ton of Cloves. A bit over two tons of Nutmeg and Cinnamon, and seven tons of tea. At first light on the morrow we set sail bor home waters.

TWELVE
FUTURES *

Samuel, nor Timothy had, had time to devote their skills to their carvings during the loading of cargo, so it was relaxing to get back to it when they were underway, off watch and, on the way home. Often some of the more meaningful conversations between Timothy and Samuel were at the change of the watch when the starboard watch crew took over running the ship from the Port watch. Or the reverse of that situation.

Others thought that the two Bosuns were just passing along information as to how the ship was behaving, or expected weather conditions concerning the amount of canvas they were carrying aloft. Perhaps even the crews moral, or health for that matter and their ability to perform their duties, but, that would not always be the topics of their talks. As they drew closer to their home port they began to talk about the shop they expected to open and potential tradesman and shopkeepers they might become. It was an awesome way to think for two men who had spent their lives on ships working for others. They were considering taking on apprentices to help with the work of basic carving, not only teaching them a possible trade, but also to help produce more wares for them to sell in the shop, or, perhaps in the market place. Both men were making mental lists of things they wanted to try and to explore in their new lives that they were about to begin.

THIRTEEN
TOOLS ✶

Three days into their voyage homeward bound, Samuel met with Smokey, the ship's blacksmith in his corner of the shop he shared with Chips the ships carpenter.. Samuel knew some of Smokey's history and that he had served for the Royal service for a time. Also that he had knowledge of making fine instruments for the Naval surgeons. They were alone in the blacksmiths shop as Samuel asked. "Smokey, can you make me some fine saws and knives like the Royal Surgeons use?"

Smokey was surprised by the question. Not many knew of his past. And his abilities for finer detailed works. "Aye, I could if need be."

Samuel handed over a fine tooth saw that he used in cutting Ivory and also two small fine Knives he used a great deal. "If you could find the time before we reach home, to make me several like these, I can put a few pounds into your hands for your efforts."

Smokey took hold of the carvers tools and looked at them for several seconds. Examining each carefully. It would take all of his skills to make fine knives and saws like these, and time as well. Finally he answered. "A few pounds you say?"

"If you can make them like these, aye a few pounds it is but it will be paid out to you after we are back ashore and we are paid off by the Captain as I've not the funds with me."

Smokey was not concerned with payment he knew Samuel to be a man of his word.

FOURTEEN
WEATHER ✶

The voyage homeward went easily for the most part. The ship was heavily loaded with cargo so she was a steady deck to work on. The crew's health was decent as they had, had enough fruits and vegetables to ward off the scurvy. They'd also been lucky enough to avoid cockroaches and fleas aboard, and the molasses was not infected with bugs of any sort. This was all due to the careful overseeing the meals prepared by the ships cook. Still it seemed as though it had been a year since they had left the Spice Islands, but it had only been just over three months. The captain expected to sight land at any time now.

As one of the last days at sea, the sky started to turn ugly. There was no question a storm was brewing behind them and it was catching up with them. The captain and mates were on the quarterdeck watching the port watch helmsman 'Benjamin' who was beginning to struggle with the ship's wheel. Samuel, the Bosun was helping him when needed, but it was clear he was going to have to have another member of the Port watch with him on the wheel.

"Mister Mirelles, We need to shorten sail. Furl the mains and topsail. Lets run under double reefed Spanker and reefed jibs. That'l slow her down some and make her easier to handle."

"Aye, Sir."

38

"You and Mister Mason might want to be ready to heave her to if she goes to fast. We're close to home and we surely don't want to end up on the Scilly Islands."

"Aye, aye, Sir' I'll keep the crews ready to heave to on your orders, Sir."

"Mister Mirelles. You're a man of the sea and you have been through a good many storms. If you feel uncomfortable with the ship's behavior, don't wait for me to give the order. Get it started man, and send a messenger to my cabin to let me know at the time."

In less than three hours time, the two mates had done exactly that. Then they let any crewmen not needed on deck, to go below and get any rest they could. It was understood that they could be called on deck at any time. By late the next morning the storm had worked its way past them and they were closing on the land before them. It had been a well thought out plan to heave to during the night. To have done otherwise may have cost them all their lives. Less than a turn of the sand glass later, a cry from the masthead. "Land ho. . . off the Port bow."

The first mate had sent Samuel below to pass the word to the captain. It was only a few minutes before the captain, the first and second mates as well as both Bosuns were on the quarterdeck looking forward to see if the land had come into view.

Though captain Neuman understood it would be a spell before that happened. He knew the masthead was seventy-five feet above the main deck and would give the lookout the ability to see much farther ahead than those of them at deck level. He spoke up now. "Mister Mason. We'll change course on your watch. That will be about four turns of the sand glass. Give her room Mister Mason. Don't crowd the turn toward home. And send word to me just before you make a change in the course and too come about."

The second mate didn't know how the captain could know when they were going to be ready to change the ships course and make the turn toward their home port in four hours. But then he was not a navigator, as was the captain. His reply came as. "Aye, sir."

When Captain Neuman was once again on deck, Young John was at his side as they stood leaning against the Port rail of the quarter deck looking ahead at the land just ahead. There was not a soul below deck. Everyone was topside. The excitement of being this close to home in nearly a year was an overwhelming feeling. The Spanker and jibs had, had their reefing ties removed and pulling the ship well ahead. They hd been on a Starboard reach, but now they were on a Port reach. The main and mizzen were unfurled with the yards braced around for the new course and, The 'John T. Franklin' had picked up a knot in her speed. As if the ship knew it was close to home, and a needed period of rest.

FIFTEEN
HOME PORT *

They made their way into the bay during the dark of night and dropped the anchor as close to the Humphry wharf as they could and still remain safely anchored during the overnight stay. On the Starboard watch, The first mate had the captain's skiff put over the side and ready for his use. At six bells the Captain climbed down the Jacobs ladder and his boat crew took him ashore. Word was out and the docks were already full of townspeople who had relatives on the ship and were just waiting until the ship would be pulled to the wharf and secured for its stay in port while its cargo was removed.

Within the hour Mister Humphry had arranged for two long boats to bring the ship along side the wharf. This saved the John T. Franklin crew still on board from having to do that themselves. Lines were passed down to the boat crews who secured them to a tow cleat on each boat. The anchor was brought aboard and the helmsman in each long boat called out for the men aboard to pull at their oars. Once the ship began to move, she moved slowly and her course was directed by the helmsman, Jeffery, who swung the stern to the wharf at the last minute as the stern lines were tossed to waiting dockhands. Her sluggish movement through the water came to a halt as the tension in the cleated dock lines came taunt.

Even then it was another two hours before anyone was allowed to board the ship as the crew was securing the rigging and putting the ship in order. Then as the crew left the ship a clerk from Humphry's shipping company office passed the word they were to come back aboard on the morrow to be paid off, that, or they could wait and take a share of the profits from the goods the ship had brought home. The crew in general would take the wages as it could take weeks, or even months before all of the spices had been sold and the total monies counted. Mister Humphry knew from experience that the ship's crew would be wanting to leave the ship and go to their families, so it would be best if he had the men from his warehouse unload the ship's cargo and move the goods to one of his ware houses.

As Samuel was leaving the ship, the clerk said to him. "Mister Bowman, Mister Humphry would like you to join him at his office at your convenience."

"Aye, and thank him if you will. I'll come by on the morrow."

"As you say, sir."

Timothy, who was right behind Samuel, said after they reached the bottom of the gangplank."At your convenience Mister Bowman." He was smiling as he looked at Samuel.

You should come along Tim. I think it might interest you as well."

SIXTEEN
SHOP ✱
Late the following morning the two men entered the outer
office of Humphry Limited. Martin, Mister Humphry'
secretary, who had been with him for many years, led them to
his office. Inside Richard rose to greet them, but was
surprised to see Mister Rollins, one of the ship's Boatswains
as well. He offered them seats, then they talked briefly about
the voyage for a few minutes. Finally Richard got down to
business. He just assumed it was okay to get into this part of
their visit with Timothy in attendance.

"Samuel. There is a shop of a good size I think will work for
your needs and it's just a short distance from "The Queen's
Inn." I've drawn you a map of where it's to be found so that
you can look at it and make a decision as to its location and
what we talked about before you left those many months
ago."

As he handed Samuel the map, he also handed him a slip of
paper with the amount it would cost to use it monthly, or to
purchase it outright. It was but a short while later that the two
men were on the roof covered deck in the front of the
building unlocking the front door to a shop. To their delight
they also found it had two apartments that took up the entire
second floor upstairs. Only as hallway separated the two
apartments which were across a narrow hall from each other..
This would allow them their own separate quarters with ease
to the shop below. Each man's quarters had a small heating

stove that could also be used to cook limited meals on, or making a pot of tea when desired. They were also surprised to find one of the newest kinds of beds were in place. They were not roped supported mattresses, they had what was being called, 'bed springs.' Also downstairs at the back of the shop was a large room that could accommodate a decent work shop and a with ample room for others who might be employed. A larger rear door was apparently used for receiving goods that were to be delivered to the shop as needed and it too had a covered deck attached to the builing..

Late afternoon Timothy was moving his, and Samuels belongings from the ship into their shop apartments, while Samuel was taking care of the financial matters of the shop with Mister Humphry. Money had been exchanged for payment of the shop from the funds of the previous sale of the expensive Ivory chess set Samuel had sold to Richard. Before the voyage. The shop was now his to use as he wished.

It was several days of ongoing work but finally the shop was of use. Samuel had gone back to the ship and had given Smokey the pounds sterling he had agreed to pay for the new tools. He also had a meeting with Chips. Where a fee was agreed upon and it did not take long before there were four small tables with rough chairs in the shop's front area. A place where chess players could gather to play chess. And in the back room three work benches had been built for Sam and Tim's needs. Shelves had been made from ship planking that had weathered, but were not overly rough. It was a hastily assembled shop, but they planned on fixing it up, and adding to it as the monies came to them. Now, they could sell their wares and get word out that, they were here and the wares they would sell. That and with offers of chess games to be played. Samuel would start spending a little time at "The Queens Inn" and pass around word where there was a fine place for chess players to gather for a game, or two. And Timothy would start working the docks and shops around that area for contacts who might have access to the things he and Sam needed.

SEVENTEEN
THE TWINS ✶

Martin, Mister Humphry's secretary, had stopped by the shop and mentioned that Richard would like a word with Samuel at his convenience. So, on this day, mid week, Samuel had gone to Richards office. The meeting of the two men had been casual, as if just a normal visit. The meeting took place as if one had dropped in on the other for a few moments. Then out of the blue, Richard said. "Samuel, I have two family members that show possible talent with sculpting, and have an interest in carving and the like. But, they have no one to guide them properly. I was wondering if you might be interested in speaking with them to determine of they have any talent? If so I could pay you a fee for them as apprentices."

It did not take Samuel any time to answer. He was in this man's debt for his help over the past many months. "Sir, it would pleasure me to be of some help, and guidance if I can do so."

"I could have them drop by in two days in the early afternoon, if that suits you?"

Samuel replied "You said two of them"?

"Oh, yes. Did I mention that they are twins."

Two days later, Samuel and Timothy were in the store front, and checking their wares for sale as well as rearranging three more chess tables they had acquired, but were really waiting for Richard's family members to arrive. The two men were currently discussing a display of scrimshaw when the bell over the shop's door tinkled indicating someone had come inside. They turned to look toward the door, and were met by the very pleasant sight of two young women. There was no question they were twins. Quietly Tim muttered, "Oh my lord. What do we have here?"

The nearest woman, who was apparently not timid and not afraid to speak up, said. "I'm Sara, and this is my sister Susan. Our uncle mentioned you might be able to help us learn how to keep our hands busy in our interests of carving?"

Both men were struck by the enormity of what lie ahead of them. The fact that two attractive women were to become apprentices was going to be a constant challenge. Samuel came to greet them first and said. "I could fix some tea and we can sit at a chess table to chat and go over what it is you already know and what we might help you with."

And so it began. The lives of these four people would never be the same again.

EIGHTEEN
JESSELYN *

It was late morning and Timothy was arranging the horn for display that he had been working on for some time with the scrimshaw mermaid adorning its side, in the window of the shop. Samuel had been in the back in the workroom going over some carving details with the twins, when the bell over the door, tinkled its melodious sound. Shortly Timothy poked his head through the door and said. "Sam. There's someone here you need to speak with."

As Samuel entered the front of the shop he saw her. It had been sometime past since he'd seen her last, but they knew each other. He held out his hand in welcoming her. "Jesselyn, you look wonderful."

"Samuel, you've changed little as well."

He felt she was not here to just visit. He felt she had a purpose in mind. "How can I help you, Jesselyn?"

"I've come about my son John. He wishes to come here to play chess. Often, I'm afraid."

Samuel's mind brought forth a mental picture of the lad he'd started teaching how to play chess not long past. "He's a good lad, Jesselyn. The lad is welcome at any time, Jesselyn. Any time."

"You would see to his well being, Samuel?"

"He would come of no harm here with us. I'm sure of that. Though I thought he was apprenticed to Captain Neuman?"

"He is, But the 'John T. Franklin' is on the hard for some time. And John would like to fill that time here with you and Mister Rollins."

"We welcome him whenever he is able to join us." Then he ventured. "When might we expect him?"

"On the morrow, if that would be fine with you?"

Samuel smiled, and said. "We'll even see that he eats a meal now and then."

After Jesselyn had left the shop Tim asked. "Is that young John's mum?"

"It is. She's had a few squalls in her life, but she's a good woman."

"A storm or two you say?"

"Aye. She is the mistress to Reginald Bowers. The ships pilot who is also a chart maker.".

NINETEEN
NEW DESIGNS ✻
It had been several weeks since Sara and Susan had come
into the shop to learn how to carve chess pieces, and to learn
the art of scrimshaw, and they had done well. Sara had been
drawn to the carving of chess pieces and Susan had found
scrimshaw more to her liking To the point that one morning
Sara asked Samuel for a moment to hear of her new idea. He
sat now, next to her at her work bench, listening. He could
smell the sweetness of her and it stirred him in ways he had
not felt in some time.

She started with. "Chess sets are for wealthy people, they
simply cost to much for most others to have as possessions.
So, I thought that if we could save carving time and
materials, we could sell them for less."
Intrigued, he asked. "How would we do this?"

"The Knights are a good example. To carve the Knight on
horseback, with his broadsword and shield, take me a great
deal of time. Why could we not just carve a plain horses head
instead. Every player would understand what it was meant to
be. Then the Bishop in all of their finery, could simply be a
Mitre hat on a pedestal, or on a small round table. The Queen
could be standing instead of seated on her throne. The King
could still be standing, but without a broadsword or scepter
staff in his hands. The Rooks could just become a siege
towers, which is much easier to carve. Pawns could be simple
round pieces, without much adornment. I mean they are just

50

little more than castle guards as it were." Samuel was trying to see these chess pieces in his mind, and made the decision to try out her idea. "Okay, Sara. Use some of our more simple woods and make a set to have a look at, and to get others to tell us what they think about these new chess men. And then we'll have to come up with a price that makes them more tempting to spend one's money on and to have in their possession."

Sara continued with."We'll also need a few more tools, and one of those lathe things. You know for turning chess pieces and for the pegs for the traveling chess sets."

"A lathe?" He knew of lathes, but had not considered their use here in the shop.

"Yes. You use it like a treadle spinning wheel. It's for turning wood and you use a wood cutting knife to cut away the wood you want to take off. In our case leaving the chess piece you want."

Samuel was surprised at her knowledge of such things, and merely said. "And where am I to get one of these lathe tools for you?'

She smiled as she replied. "I'll see to it Sam."

Again he was surprised. She had called him Sam, not Samuel. Interesting he thought.

TWENTY
SHANDY ✻

Timothy and Samuel were at 'The Queen's Inn' having a pint of Ale, and as they spoke about how things were going, a man came into the Inn, looked around and saw the two of them. He headed in their direction ans as he drew near, he spoke to the two of them. He was looking at Sam as he did so. "Bones, words out on the wharf that you and Scrimshander there wanted to speak to me."

"Aye, that we do. Sit, if you will?"

As Shandy pulled up a chair and sat. Tim held up his hand so the woman behind the bar rail could see him. He held up one finger, pointed to his pint, then to Shandy. In moments she sat a pint of Ale down in front of him and he thanked her. They had known of him from the docks when the two of them had been shipmates on the John T. Franklin. They also knew he had contacts everywhere in the area. That was exactly why they had let it be known around the docks that they would like to have a word with him. They took a few minutes to explain what it was they were in need of, then waited for his reply.

"So. You gentlemen want me to find all kinds of Fancy woods or other different woods, but more hardwoods than soft. Like Teak and Rosewood, even Mahogany. You want Ivory and Walrus tusks, and things like that kind of stuff as well?"

Timothy raised a finger and said. "Aye, and you might keep an eye out for most any whale bones and teeth of the sperm whale. Even Stag antlers or horns of any kind.".

"Well now, mates. How do I come by the funds for these things you are asking me to find?

Samuel and Timothy both knew this was something they would have to deal with. They had inquired as to Shandy's reputation, and for the most part he was honest in his dealings. Shady as they might be. They knew as well that he would always came away with a few shillings for his trouble.

"If you find something you think will be what we need, try to argue a price that you think is a good price. Then come see if we are willing to take a chance on the price for the goods, If so, we'll give you the funds you need. If this works out for all of us, we'll see that you have some monies to work with, but you'll have to account for what monies you pay out."

"How many times will you need me for these things?"

Timothy said. " Perhaps for years if you can get us what we need. And as you may be aware, most Ivory comes from Norway or Sweden. "

"I know a few ships carpenters who often have many kinds of wood. I'll ask around, and I'll start on the morrow."

TWENTY ONE
WAGERS ✭

Many of the Towne's chess players had found the new chess club by now, so it was no longer a surprise when someone entered the shop. Today's visitor, a well dressed gentleman entered and as he did so the bell over the door tinkled softly. He passed by a chess table he saw young John sitting at the table, seemingly just looking at the board and fingering the chess pieces on chess board. He hesitated along the side the table for a moment, and said. "You play chess young lad?"

John looked up and with a face of innocence, replied. "I know how the pieces move. Sir."

The man smiled as he pulled a chair up to the table, and moved the white King's Pawn two spaces. John's fingers touched the King's Knight pawn, then started to pull his fingers back as if embarrassed by this possible chess move, but then he continued by moving the King's Knight Pawn out two spaces. The man looked at John, as if appraising him, then said. "Do wager your games, Lad." Not actually expecting a reply.

John tried to look confused as he said. "Wager my games. Sir?

Samuel, standing nearby was listening to the two of them and said. "The Lad doesn't wager his games, but I'd be interested in doing so. What wager do you have in mind, sir?"

"A pound, I win the game." Now, he turned more serious at the thought of playing chess with this young lad and making a pound or two as well.

Samuel looked quickly to John, as if he too was appraising the boy. Unseen by the man across the table by him, John made a quick but slight nod of his head, and Samuel said. "So be it. A pound it is."

The man's next move was the Queens Pawn out one square. John followed this by moving his King's Bishop's Pawn out one square as if to protect the Knights Pawn The man smiled and moved his Queen to his King's Rook five and said. "I believe that's checkmate Lad."

John just gave a loud sigh, tilted his head downward and was quiet a moment, then said. "Perhaps I could do better next time."

The man looked to Samuel, and said. "I've won a pound, do you favor the loss of another?"

Again John nodded when the man was looking at Samuel. Samuel stalled a moment or two, and finally agreed to a wager of another pound. "So be it."

This time the gentleman played white again and moved the King's Pawn two spaces. John did the same with his King's pawn. Then the man moved his King's Bishop to the Queen's

Bishop four square. John then moved his Queen's Pawn out one square. His opponent then moved his Queen to his King's Bishop three square. John moved his Queen's Knight to the Queen's Bishop three square. Quickly the man moved his Queen down to capture the black King's Bishop's Pawn and smiling broadly, said. "Again it's checkmate lad.

John seemed saddened and meekly said. "Perhaps I could try one more game, sir?"

The gentleman said. "Surely you jest young fellow?"

"I can do better, I think?"

The man looked once again to Samuel, who said. "You've won two pounds, sir. I'd like a chance to get that back."

Self confidence was oozing out of the man as he said. "How about a five pound note then."

"Well, that would get me back the two pounds, but is it worth doing so for only three pounds. I think not."

Without hesitation the man came back with. "Ten pounds, if you can?"

Samuel hesitated, but only briefly. "You have the funds do you sir?" He knew fully well this gentleman was someone of some wealth, but wanted to test his mettle, as it were.

"I do indeed." He reached into his pocket and from within his pocket purse he extracted a ten pound note and put it on a table near Samuel. Where upon Samuel as he searched his pockets finally found a five pound note and five one pound notes. He then also put them with the ten pound note on the table.

"As a chess player, you might give the lad a choice of hands, sir"

"As you say, a courtesy of course." As he turned back to face John sitting across the table he picked up a white pawn with his right hand and a black one with his left hand as well. He reached behind his back to mix them up, not knowing Young John was watching and counting the numbers in his head. As the gentleman's hands came out before him John knew from his counting that the white pawn was still in the same hand where it had started it's journey even though it had been passed from one hand to the other and back again. When the hand he chose was opened he was rewarded with the white pawn as it was being passed to him each of them knowing those pieces were his to play.

He started with the King's Pawn move to the King's four square, His opponent did the same. John then move his King's Knight to the King's Bishop three square. The man moved his Queen's Pawn out one square to protect his King's pawn. John next moved his King's Bishop to the Queen's Bishop four square. The black Bishop quickly found its way across the board to the black King's Knight five square thus pinning the white Knight. John, as if in a qaundry, moved his Queen's Knight to the Queen's Bishop four square. The gentleman then moved his Queen's Knight out to the Queen's Bishop's three square. John began to reach out, and his fingers touched his King's Knight. Then he withdrew his hand and sat still. His opponent asked. "Do you not play by the touch move rule, Lad?"

John sighed quietly, then answered. "Yes, Sir." And he picked up the knight and captured the black King's Pawn. Without hesitation the man picked up his white Bishop and captured the white Queen which was still on her home square. He knew the white King could now capture his Bishop, but was surprised when John moved his white Bishop down to capture the black Kings Bishop's Pawn and said. "Check."

There was stunned silence while the man contemplated his next move, but he had no choice but to move his King out one square, only to find John's next move, the white Queen's Knight, was moved to his Queen's four square and John announced. "Checkmate. Sir."

After the gentleman left the shop Samuel called John to the table where he had been sitting watching the game. He had the money in front of him as he said. "John of the ten pounds the gentleman lost in his last wager, I'll take three pounds to replace the loss from the first two games. Then I'll take two more for the shop. That'll leaved five pounds for yourself. Is that a fair shake of the funds?"

John was silent for a few moments, then he said. "Samuel, I've never had that much money in my whole life. What will I do with it?"

"I think you might share it with your mum, Lad. I'm sure she would be thankful."

"I could get rich playing chess couldn't I?"

There was no hesitation. "No, John. Chess players never get rich from playing chess. Never."

TWENTY TWO
CHESS MASTER ✶

A magnificently whiskered man wearing a top coat and top hat entered the shop. He spoke quietly with both Samuel and Timothy. His words were those used by the upper class of wealthy people around the towne. But, as it turns out he introduced himself as 'William Harwick' of Surrey, a man with a known reputation as a master chess player. After the three of them had finished introducing themselves to one another, Samuel invited him to a game of chess. Which, of course William won handily. Samuel didn't like to lose, but of course, no one does. Still, he was impressed with Williams understanding of the game and his innate ability to foresee many moves ahead as to what might take place. A question came to Samuel's mind and he asked. "How long have you played this game of chess, sir?"

"Samuel. You needn't call me, Sir. William will do just fine. And, as it happens, my father taught me the game when I was a lad of six. I've since studied it closely."

As they spoke of the game just played, and moves where some plays might have been better having been left alone at the time. Then William said."My friend, Sir Hamilton, the Earl, suggested I come by your shop. He spoke highly of you and the young lad who was here during his visit to your shop"

Sam couldn't believe his ears. "The Earl, Sir Hamilton said he was here?"

"Yes he mentioned losing ten pounds to a young fellow. John, I think he said?"

Sam was now concerned because of how that chess game had taken place. "Was the Earl upset with young John?"

"Oh, no. Not at all. In fact I believe you will see more of Earl Hamulton and his friends here from time to time. You've a different kind of shop Samuel, a chess club if you will. There's few of these around."

TWENTY THREE
LESSONS *

William Harwick had dropped into the chess club one afternoon just a bit before young John arrived. When John arrived Samuel had introduced them to one another and a chess game had come about. It surprised Samuel at how long the two of them had sat at one of the now seven tables in a far corner. The two of them were deep into conversations and he didn't want to interrupt them. It seems as if William was showing John several chess game openings and John was paying close attention. After a lengthy time John had to take his leave, and William came to Samuel. "That boy has a quick mind. He pulls in knowledge like a dry cloth. He knows his numbers better than any other man I've ever done business with as of late. Mark my word, he'll be a champion one day."

Samuel was remembering what he'd told John about never getting rich playing chess as he said. "He's got no one to teach him enough to become a champion."

"Oh, but he does. Me."

TWENTY FOUR
CHESS MEN ✫

There had been a day mid week that had started out busy in the shop. Jesselyn had come in with her son John, then a few of chess players had arrived at the nearly the same time as well. To the point that Samuel was busy collecting fees from the players who wanted to use one of his new chess sets to play a few games at one of the tables in the club's open room. Some of the fee. would be returned to them set when they were finished with the chess set for the day. He was so busy that he'd simply lost all tract of time and Jesselyn's where abouts as well. He wasn't aware she had spent most of her time in the back work room of the shop with Sara and Susan.

As he and Tim were closing the shop at the end of day, Sara called out to him. "Samuel, come have a look if you please."

As he entered the back room and moved near her, she said. "A moment if you will, please I need to finish this one first."

He watched as Sara was putting the final touches to the carving of a Knight. Her hands moving swiftly as she wielded the small and very sharp knife deftly with her fingers and as she peeled away small slivers of wood to reveal the neck of the horse's head on the chess piece. Another cut or two and it was nearly finished. It needed only to have some stain applied, then a coat of varnish.

Setting her things aside, She led him to another work bench and pointed to quite a number of unfinished Pawns lying on the surface. He could see it would take very little time to finish any carving they might require, then to stain them as needed. Then she said. "Jesselyn made these today on our new lathe."

"She made all of these in one day?"

"Yes. She's quite handy, she is., and I'll teach her how to make the Bishops next"

His mind racing at the prospect of a quicker way to make chessmen, it was indeed a blessing. "Maybe we should think about asking her to spend more time here in the shop."

"Oh, Sam. I've already done so. I hope you don't mind. You see, with her help and the new kind of chess pieces we are making. I can bring new chess sets to you much more often."

He had been very pleased with her recent suggestions about the style of chess piece, and so were those who came looking for chess sets because the costs becoming within reach for many of the Townes gentlemen..

TWENTY FIVE
CHANGES *

Sara and Susan had been slowly making suggestions to
Samuel and Timothy about their fashion of dress. That
perhaps they should start dressing more like prosperous
shopkeepers. Even then it had taken a while but the two men
were not longer wearing the clothing of a ships crewmen.
Doing so it had, had an affect that surprised the two men
themselves when they had started this change in clothing and
bathing habits. An example had come about one day after the
chess club was closed for the day and as they had entered
"The Queen's Inn" in the early evening.

The lass who serves mugs of ale and vittles had said to them.
"Evening, Sirs. I can get you a table cleared and have you
settled shortly." She had never called them, sirs, before. Even
some of the regular group who spent time here who knew
them had stayed away and avoided speaking with them until
they called out to a forecastle hand they had spent time with
on the 'John T. Franklin."

He too had been surprises when he realized who it was
offering him a pint of Ale. As the evening passed they were
joined by a few others as well. Each man envious of Samuel
and Timothy's success.

The two men had steered the conversation around to things
they were in need of. Each of the men who was in their
company would in time bring something of value for the

shop. Things they would gather during their travels on various ships going to unknown ports of the world as they knew it. Returning it to the chess shop and in turn earn a profit making it worth their while.

TWENTY SIX ✶
THE CHALLENGE

A year or more had passed since the "Chess" shop had opened. It had become well known and the amount of chess players in attendance had increased many times over. There were days when the shop was full of chess players and others had turned away because of the lack of space for them to even watch games in play. John played on occasion and on special request, but had mentioned to Samuel. "I wish to play more often, Samuel. Still there are some who don't play chess with me as they know they can't win."

Samuel had thought about this kind of thing for some time. So he asked. "Would you like to play many games at the same time?"

"I don't know what you are asking me?"

"We now have eight tables so we could sit two players at a table, which would be ten and six players ready to play chess. You could walk to and from each player, each would have a chess set ready for your move, and after you make a your move you could go to the next table. It would be a steady voyage until each game was won or lost."

John smiled as he thought about this kind of challenge to his chess ability. He was silent for some time. Samuel did not query him again. He just waited. He knew this would tax the boys' mind some.

Then, the replay came. "Yes. If I can have William here waiting with you so that if I have a question and I need an answer for a problem."

Samuel knew that William Harwick would not miss the event he had in mind. "I'll see to it lad. That and we'll charge a fee for each player as well. The purse to be yours except for a small shop fee from each player as well for the use of our chess sets."

Still, as the idea of a simultaneous tournament for John was discussed between Samuel and Timothy and in the presence of Sara and Susan as well as Jesselyn, Jesselyn said. "John has told me many a time that chess players he has spoken with would like to have a real chess tournament. Perhaps you could do that first to see if many come to play?"

It was quiet for a spell as the enormity of that kind of event taking place here was spell binding.

Sara spoke first. "That's a splendid idea, Jesselyn. Just splendid."

And, so it began.

TWENTY SEVEN
THE SAILOR'S REST ✶
It had been the late afternoon when Shandy had come into the shop. He'd explained to Samuel.
"He's a ship's carpenter and he's just in from a voyage. He's a bloke I've had a talk with before about things for your shop. Now he's got some fine wood with him, but he's not keen on my offer to pay him. He wants to have a palaver with you."

"Where's he to be found, Shandy?"

"He's a room at the, 'Sailor's Rest."

After Shandy had left the shop Samuel had a thought, he'd take Sara with him. He went to Sara's carving bench in the back shop and pleasantly surprised to see Jesselyn working on the lathe. Standing along side Sara, he asked her. "I've got to go see a sailor about some wood he may have for us if we pay his price. Would you like to go along with me."

His asking her along was in itself a surprise, but this would be an adventure of a different kind. "Surely, I'll go with you."

It was but a short time later that Samuel and Sara stood outside the ramshackle of a building. He looked to her as he said. "Sara, this is not a tidy place. If it displeases you I can come back on the morrow."

It pleased her that he was concerned with her well being, she answered. "Samuel, I'm with you and I've no problem with this place if you can safely go inside, as can I."

He took Sara's hand in his as if to guide her when they entered the 'Sailor's Rest.' An establishment used by sailors between ships. It was cheap and you could tell that from the way it appeared unkept and untidy. Smelling of men who were unwashed and often suffering from drunken bouts from the Ale they had consumed in quantities that was not kind to their bodies. Samuel had inquired of the old woman who was the Inn keeper as to the where abouts of the ships carpenter, one of the sailors staying here. He was given directions to the man's room, but nothing more.

At his door a knock from Samuel brought a response of "Who's at there?"

"Samuel from the 'Chess' shop.

The door was unlatched and swung open. He bid them to enter and was surprised when a woman followed in behind Samuel. Their hands had parted but the feeling it had caused between them stayed firmly in their minds. A pleasure neither of them had not felt in a great while.

He was embarrassed by the way his room was in such a mess, a woman would not have allowed him to leave it this way, so without a word he just pointed to some wood atop a table.

Sara followed Sam to the table and she looked at the wood with a wood carver's eyes. As did Samuel. There was no question it was close grained white wood of high quality.

The grain was straight and true, small pores as if grown in a dry area over the years. And a quantity of which they might not come into again for some time. Samuel caught Sara's eye and winked. Then he turned to the ships carpenter.

"How is it you came by this wood."

"We'uns were in Portugal for wines and I came across this here wood. It seemed a good wood so I had it delivered to the ship's carpenter's work shop."

Samuel felt he knew what had happened. The ship would have been charged with the payment of the wood, but he said nothing about this at the moment. "What price did Shandy offer you for this wood.?"

What the sailor told him did not surprise Samuel. He just nodded and said. "Well it is a white wood, and I can use it, but the quality is less than we use most often. Still, it is better than nothing. I'm willing to pay you what shandy offered, and two shillings. If you'll be so kind as to bring it to the shop yourself."

The carpenter wanted more for the wood and he thought it to be a good wood. Still he had no use for it himself, so he agreed to the conditions. It hadn't cost him so much as a farthing.

It had been late in the day, nearly dark out when the wood was delivered to the back door of the shop, that and the price paid for it was below what the wood was really worth. This was known only to Sam and Sara.

Samuel wanted to hold Sara's hand again. As did she.

TWENTY EIGHT ★
THE FIRST TOURNAMENT

It was now known that the gentry who often played chess at the chess club had voiced their feelings often. Samuel and Timothy were following through with the idea they had talked about with the ladies after hours. That the offering of a chess tournament taking place in their establishment would be tried. If it had not been for those who frequented the club to play chess, they would have never thought about on their own. They knew it would increase business so they had decided to get the word out into the entire King's realm. They would offer a chess set as one of the prizes, and a small purse as well. It was planned for the following month's end. A two day event, or more depending on how many players were to attend and play in the games.

It became known that those who came by the chess club and paid their fee early, would be the first to play in the tournament as well. William Harwick had taken the time to explain to Samuel what kind of chess tournament to hold, and had then offered to be one to overlook the way it took place, and to enforce the rules of play. It was to be a 'One life Tournament' If a chess player lost a game, their tournament life was over. To continue in the tournament they had to win each game they played.

On the day of the tournament there was not a room available for travelers any where nearby. The Queen's Inn had been full two days prior, and the "Sailor's Rest was also full. Many players from outside the area seemed to find themselves as guests of one or more of their more wealthy friends. Rumor had been passed along that they were practicing their chess games as often as they could. Timothy had come up with two more tables and they had been crowded into the room, but there was not enough chess sets available. Fortunately Samuel and Timothy had offered a slight difference in fees for those who came with their own chess set. Not much off, but some.

It started early morning. At two bells. William called out to them. "Gentlemen, your attention if you please."

Every man turned to face him. Those at the eight tables who had chess sets set up ready to play, and those who were just standing along the walls of the room Kibitzers one and all. Most of them were on the list for the second round of games. Two tables had men who had brought their own chess sets, they too, were ready to play, but they would be in the second tournament. All in all, there were sixteen men who were nervous, but willing chess enthusiasts.

"The rules of the games are this. If you win your game you move on to the next round of play, and are still in the tournament. If you lose your game, your day is done. The length of time you have to play your game is one turn of the sand glass. If your game is not finished, I will look at the board and decide the winner of the game. The games will continue until we are down to one winner. That winner will wait and play the winner if the next round of chess players who are present and waiting for the second half of the tournament to begin."

"You should all be aware of the touch move rule, so I won't go into that. If a question comes up during your game, raise your hand and I'll come to your table to listen to your query. You must also remember that my decisions are final and will not be altered. Also, you should expect this first tournament will last nearly four hours, or six bells on board a ship as it were."

"One last thing. At the moment we have a young lad who seems a promising chess talent, and whom will hold a 'Simultaneous chess match within the next few weeks, or so. Those of you who think they can beat a young lad at a game of chess, might want to ask about playing in this tournament as well."

TWENTY NINE ★
THE SECOND TOURNAMENT

It was late afternoon before the second group of challengers finished their games. Then the two winners for both tournaments met at the chess board to do battle. The room was still crowded with onlookers. A feverous pitch of curiosity hung in the air like St. Elmos fire Even those not playing were nervous. As the games were played you could hear groans from the bystanders as one move or another was played. Some plays seemed brilliant, some daring, but most were carefully thought out before a hand reached out to move a chess piece. The game lasted for thirty eight moves before defeat was acknowledged with a King being tipped to its side.

Before the evening came entirely to an end, a first prize of seven pounds and one of Sara and Susan's new chess sets had been given to the winner. A second prize was five pounds, and a third was for three pounds but that had been the entry fee charged to play in the tournament to begin with.

Samuel had a list of the names of all of the players and their placement in the tournament standings. He was going to have Sara make him a sign with the names of the top four men in the tournament and a separate sign with the name of the champion. He would then put them on the walls of the main playing room.

THIRTY ★
THE SIMULTANEOUS TOURNAMENT
Nine players from the One life tournament had signed up to play in the simultaneous event against young John. It was to be held mid day, and Jesselyn would be present as well. Sam knew she would sit quietly over near him, but he also knew she would be very nervous as well. The baker from a few shops away had stopped in the day after the last tournament and had brought sweet breads and biscuits for everyone in the chess club group. He had explained that those who came to play chess often stopped in his shop for things to eat while having tea as well. He had explained that during the last tournament over the last couple of days had found him selling entirely all of his entire wares at the time. With that in mind Timothy had invited him to stop during the upcoming simultaneous tournament to offer his wares to those in attendance.

At eight bells and with the sun high overhead, John himself was becoming nervous. But, William was assuring him that he would get over those feeling when the games started. In fact that he would forget everything else that was going on around him. When the last of the challengers were seated at separate tables, William explained the rules of play to them. John would play white and after making his move they could decide what move they were going to make, but could not make that move until John returned to their table to see the move made at that time.

Any questions concerning the outcome of the games would be asked of him, as the tournament director, and his decision was final.

Any one who opposed this condition was free to leave now and their fee for playing would be returned to them. No one objected. And no one left.

John started at the first table and played his first move as 'e4' at the second table he played 'd4'
At the third table he played 'Nf3' at the fourth table he played 'e4' and again at the fifth table he played 'd4' with the sixth table it was again 'Nf3' this continued with each remaining tables. The games went well, and of course in his favor as his opponents had only considered him a child and not a child with a polished chess mind. At seven bells all but one player was left. The others had been beaten, not easily, but they had lost t their games non-the-less. This last game was down to an ending that would no doubt end in a draw. When finally the man sitting across from John reached out and offered his hand, John accepted the offer of a draw and the day of chess ended.

It had taken just over four hours of play to finish the last game and John was exhausted. He was also eighteen pounds richer. Nothing had been taken out of the game funds for the shops usage. They knew he had put in a tough day and had earned every shilling of the fee charged for the simultaneous match.

They did know John was tired, also very pleased with how he had done in the tournament. Maybe he'd do that again sometime. He knew for sure his mother could use the huge sum of monies he'd won from the chess games.

THIRTY ONE
PROFITS *

Late that evening Samuel and Timothy were having a pint of ale at the 'The Queen's Inn' The discussion was concerning the profits the shop had made since they had started in this endeavor in the beginning.

Timothy said. "You know, Mate. We've done well here. I'm thinking we might have enough to share with Sara, Susan and Jesselyn."

"You mean we should pay them a wage." As Samuel said this, he looked at his partner with the question in his eyes.

"I'm not sure a wage is the proper way, but , , , "

Samuel interrupted and said. "Perhaps a share in the years profits?"

"Aye, Samuel. We could parcel it out according to how many days each of them put in making chess sets, or scrimshaw works."

"How will we know that though?. I've no idea how long each of them has spent working at their benches during the year."

"I do. You see Susan has been keeping count. She doesn't know I know, but I've seen her personal time ledger. I think she keeps it as a list of times it takes her do things.

So she could tell us. If we ask."

Sam thought about it for a few moments, then added. "So, it would be shared after funds for the shop, costs of our materials. Then shares for you and I, as well, and a partial share divided between the three of them."

Timothy smiled at the thought of how happy that would make the three women. "Aye, that's about it mate."

"Okay, but let's keep this to ourselves until we have come up with how to do this. Okay?"

"Done mate. Done."

THIRTY TWO
CREW MEETING ✶
The shop had been closed for several minutes now, but the three women were waiting for Sam and Tim to tell them why they wanted them to stay over for a few minutes.

Finally Sam said. "Ladies, have a seat, if you will.?"

Still nervous, they sat at two tables near each other, and Sam started explaining why they were there. "Tim and I have been figuring out how much we had left in the strong box after the costs of paying for out supplies, and things we needed to run the shop for the year."

"Because of the speed with which you three have been making chess sets, we have become known for some distance, a distance I'd not thought possible. We've had several orders for custom chess sets that Tim and I are working on, and requests for more are coming in from all over the king's realm. Perhaps further in one cor two cases. We may have to employ another person to help you three with small details you can give them and to make your chores easier. But . . . here's the thing . . ."

At this point, Tim apologized when he interrupted and then gave a rough idea of how much they had left over, which wasn't a great deal, but still it was an amount that would allow them to continue doing business.

"And, with that in mind, Sam and I have decided you three should have a share in the coming years monies. After costs, of course."

Susan asked. "Are you telling us that we will have a share of the monies that are left over after the costs are spent to keep the shop open for business this year?"

Sam, said. "Yes, that's what he means."

It seemed as though Sara was holding back tears in her eyes. It was an unheard of situation for women to have a share in a business of any kind. Well, except for one.

For a few minutes after this was explained in more detail, there was laughter and warm feelings among them. After leaving the shop, and as they were walking home. Sara said, "Susan, we should have Sam and Tim to our cottage for supper some evening. Don't you think?"

Susan smiled, she knew Sara was taken with Sam. As she was with Tim. "Yes, I'd like that."

THIRTY THREE
ROYALTY ✶

It was mid day when the magnificent coach arrived at the chess club. As it stopped in front of the chess club's door, Samuel could see a small royal emblem on the side of the coaches door. He called out to Timothy in the back before the man entered the shop. The man who came inside was dressed in very finely tailored clothing and walked in a confidential manner. Sam and Tim were speechless, but this was soon to be forgotten. Had they looked outside they would have seen every other shop keeper outside their own establishments looking in their direction to see what was going on.

"Gentlemen, I'm Reginald Thorton. I'm a representative of the Royal court and one of the Queen's envoys. To whom am I speaking?"

Sam and Tim both nervous, gave their names, then, Thorton continued. "I'm enquiring about a young person known only to me as, 'John who plays chess." Is he present?"

Before further words were spoken Samuel turned to look at Timothy and with a nod of his head he motioned toward the back room of the shop. Timothy understood exactly what Samuel wanted and he turned and opened the door to the back room and quietly said. "Jesselyn. A moment if you will?

Hurriedly Jesselyn had joined the men in the main playing room. Samuel explained to her who the man was and what he had asked.

Jesselyn, as a child's mother, then said to the Queen's envoy. "I'm John's mother. Why is it you are seeking my son?"

"Madam, I have been instructed to ask him to attend an audience with the Queen. She was advised of his ability at the chess board by the Earl Hamilton. "

Jesselyn's legs felt weak, she reached out to Timothy for support as she steadied herself. "When is he to appear?"

"On the morrow would be fine, Madam."

"My son will appear, but only if I, his mother, can accompany him?"

"As you wish, Madam. I'll send a coach for your convenience."

Upon learning of the events that were about unfold, John was not too concerned at where he and his mother were to go. It was why they were going that he on his mind. He rarely saw his mother wearing her finest clothing, nor had he a reason to wear his. Still he understood it was a high honor of sorts to be invited to the royal court.

It was four days before Jesselyn returned to the shop. As she entered the back door, even before the shop normally opened, everything that had been going on inside stopped. The questions came fast and ran together as she tried to answer them. Finally she had them understanding that John was to become a chess tutor to all of the Royal families' children. That he would be receiving a fee from the court and have his own quarters there and teach for four days, then be delivered home for four days. This to be an ongoing cycle until the Queen was satisfied, or until John had, had enough and wished to stop the chess lessons. Jesselyn was given a room for her own visits, but she had explained. "It's much to stiff and formal for the likes of me. I like coming here and spending my time with all of you."

THIRTY FOUR
MARTIN ★

When Mister Humphry's secretary entered the shop he found Samuel and Timothy talking with Chips, the ships carpenter. All three of them were surprised when they were given the message that. "The John T. Franklin is off the hard and back afloat. She's going south to Madeira for wines and I need to speak with Jesselyn about John's going along as the ships cabin boy, as before."

Sam had to smile as he informed Martin. "John will not be joining the ship for this voyage."

Martin raised an eyebrow as he asked. "Why would that be the case?"

"He's in the Queen's service."

Martin looked confused, and surprised as well. "In the Queen's service you say?"

Timothy replied. "Aye, it is so."

"Oh my word.. Lordy, lordy. Mister Humphry will be amazed I'm sure of that."

After Martin had left to report back to Mister Humphry, Chips said. "I best be getting my things ready to go. I've been at the 'Sailor's Inn' for the past days. I'll be expected to be aboard. Maybe on the morrow."

Sam asked. "Chips, keep an open eye for woods, or ivory for us if you will. And we can provide some funds if you feel the need?"

"Aye. I'll do that, but I won't be needing funds before hand. If I find things you can use, I'll get it in some way. Then you can repay me when we are back in our home port again."

THIRTY FIVE ✵
THE MEETING TABLE
It was mid morning at the chess club and everyone was
sitting at a large round table in the carving room. There was
no one waiting to play chess. Tea and sweetbreads had been
delivered by the baker's shop nearby and the discussion was
about how slow business was during this time of year when it
was wet, windy, or just plain foul. Timothy had suggested,
"Why don't we just close the shop on Mondays?"

Susan ventured her thoughts. "We could get other things
done that are difficult on normal work days." It hadn't taken
much more than that to help make the decision to do just that.
Sara placed her hand on top of Sam's and explained. "We
could take down the sign on the door that says 'It's Your
Move' and put up a sign that we would be open on the
morrow." Sam's hand tingled with excitement as her hand
covered his. Still he thought the sign idea would work out
well.

They were nearly finished with their tea when the bell over
the door chimed. It had been completely forgotten. Sam got
up and went to see who it was. When he entered the playing
room he found Shandy trying to pull a heavy canvas bag in
the door behind him. "Shandy, what it it you have there?"

"It's Ivory I've found for you, Bones. Ivory."

Timothy and Samuel helped Shandy get the bag to a work bench in the carving room where the contents were removed and placed on a bench. They were all surprised at what they found inside. It was all Walrus Ivory, but most if it was small, and some were broken pieces. Sam questioned their sizes, but Tim had been pleased with it and he explained. "The sizes are not large, but I can use most all of it to make chess pieces carved with scrimshaw figures for the chessmen."

When a price had been agreed on, Shandy had left the shop. It hadn't been ten minutes before the bell chimed again. This time it was Richard Humphry. He started with. "Samuel, a few moments of your time, if you will?"

"Surely, Richard. What can I do for you, Sir?"

"Take a walk with me. I've a surprise for you."

Sam put on a hat and coat, then went out the door with Richard. They turned toward a part of towne that Sam had been to before, but was not in the habit of frequenting. As the two men walked, Richard said. "You know Sam. When my path crosses that of Sara's, she speaks very highly of you."

"Does she now?"

"Yes she does. She's sweet on you Sam. Very much so."

Just as Sam was about to ask more about Sara's comments, Richard said. "Ahh, here we are now."

He opened the door for Sam, and as he entered the building he realized it was the 'Harbour Bank' He turned to look back at Richard, who said nothing, but just walked by him and led the way to a fine desk where the man behind it stood to greet them. He said. "Richard, good to see you again."

The two men shook hands as Richard introduced him. "Mister Hightower, this is Samuel Bowman. This time the banker reached out his hand to Sam, who took it in his own. After the introductions were over, Sam and Richard took seats near the desk and the banker said. "So, Mister Bowman I'll only need your signature on a form so that you can begin using your account."

Sam was very much surprised. "I have an account here in your bank?"

This time Richard offered. "Yes, Sam. I've taken the monies you have been keeping in my strongbox and placed it into an account in your name here at the bank."

After they had left the bank and Sam now felt like an accomplished business man, he asked. "Were my funds not safe in your strongbox, Richard.?"

"Oh, yes Quite. But Sara's suggested that you needed to belong to a businessman's bank. And she thought this bank would suit your needs. She does her banking here as well."

Now he was curious. "Sara has bank accounts here?"

"Oh, yes Sam. You see when the twins' parents passed, they were left a sizeable fortune, and the monies are kept here in this bank. The cottage of course was part of the estate as well."

"Are the twins wealthy then?"

"No, not in the sense you may be thinking, but well to do at any rate."

When Sam was back in the shops carving room, he said. "Well, now we have a banking account at the 'Harbour Bank' He noticed a large smile on Sara's face as Timothy began his query about the clubs bank account. He said not a word about her using the bank herself as well. There was no need to do so.

THIRTY SIX ✳
QUEEN'S & KINGS

Jesselyn had been hard at work, so busy in fact that no one paid much attention to what she was doing. She was turning something on the lathe, but it wasn't until she called Sara over to her work bench that the project she had been thinking about for some time was to be revealed to the others.

"Sara. Could you have a look at these and tell me what you think?"

Sara came to the turning bench and as Jesselyn handed her an object she sucked in a breath. She knew exactly what it was she had been handed. She smiled broadly and said. "A moment dear friend. A moment." She went to the door to the main playing room and as she peeked out she saw Sam speaking with two players at a chess table.

"Sam, please come into the back when you can."

She hadn't seemed to be rushing him, but there was something in her voice. He excused himself and followed her into the back room. She stopped by Jesselyn's bench and handed him what she herself had been given. He too, understood the significance of the piece of turned wood in his hand. He looked to Jesselyn and said. "You've a wonderful imagination, Jesselyn. She will take little carving to make her into the Queen she wants to become."

The wooden body was round from top to bottom. Wider at the base then narrow for a waist, outward again for the bosom, narrow once again for the neck, then a bit larger for the head and possible crown. He continued with. "And with little work to cut one of the top portions into a Queen's crown"

Then Jesselyn surprised the two of them as she handed them another turned piece. It was similar, but slightly higher in length, and had a section for the head and yet larger round bulb on the top which allowed for a cross to be cut, thus signifying his position as the ruler of the kingdom on the chess board..

Jesselyn offered. "You see, if you cut down on each side and leave a thinner slice in the center, then you can cut the rest of it into a cross. I think it would look like the King on a chess board. He wouldn't have to have a broad sword, or a scepter in his hand, the cross would tell others that he was the supreme ruler."

Sam called Tim and Susan over to the meeting table and the five of them sat down. The showing of the pieces jesselyn had made evoked the discussion that followed, which was one of curiosity, and excitement. It was decided to make four chess sets with these new designed chess pieces, and use them as the sets chess players would use when play with they came into the shop and needed to borrow a chess. Of course the fee for its use would still apply.

THIRTY SEVEN ★
SUPPER

Samuel and Timothy had been to the bath house earlier, then returned to their rooms at the shop where they had dressed in the scant few of their 'Gentlemen's' clothing. On the walk to the twins cottage, Timothy noticed that Sam seem much quieter than normal. "You feelin a storm coming on Sam?"

Sam said. "I'm a mite worried."

Tim looked at his partner, and asked. "Why, pray tell, are you worried. It's not like we are strangers to these two women?"

"I'm a bit worried about telling Sara something."

"What is it that, ... Oh, there's their cottage just ahead."

Both men had stopped to look at the cottage. "Tim this place is the size of two four masted schooners rafted together."

"It's not a piker is it?"

Susan was the one to answer the door at their knock, and when inside the two men were met with a fine household. All was in order, and everything neatly arranged. In reality neither man had ever spent any real amount of time in someone's private cottage. This one seemed magnificent to them. After a few minor greeting pleasantries, while taking their coats, and the like. Sara said.

95

"You are here just in time. Our supper is nearly ready to enjoy."

The twins led them to the dining room. Sam sat on one side of the table, and Tim on the other. The twins then disappeared for a few moments and when they returned they brought a large pot of stew to the table, that and a pot of tea as well as a loaf of bread cut into slices. The twins then seated themselves at the ends of the table.

It was quiet for a minute or two, as they partook of the meal, but then Sam said. "Ladies, I do believe this is the best meal I've ever had the pleasure of eating." He didn't know which spoon to use for his stew. There was a small one and a larger one. He looked to the twins and saw what they were using and he did the same.

Tim was also greatly impressed with the meal, and added. "Here, here."

After they had finished the meal, Susan led them to the parlor and said, "Take a seat if you will. Sara and I will be right back." Sam sat on a divan, while Tim took a chair on one side of the low parlor table. They could hear the dining table being cleared, then shortly Susan came into the parlor carrying two bottles of wine. Sara followed with a tray of crystal stem ware glasses.

Susan took a chair across from Timothy, while Sara placed the tray of glasses with the short parlor table between the two chairs and the divan. Then she joined Sam on the divan.

After the first bottle of wine had been consumed, Sam had come to the conclusion that he liked wine better than Ale at the "Queen's Inn". He was also feeling light headed. Then suddenly Tim said."Sam, what was it you were going to say to Sara?"

Samuel was flustered as the thoughts he had been thinking flashed through his mind, and now Timothy had made it apparent to the two women that Sam had something on his mind.

Sara turned to face him, and asked."You've something to tell me, Sam?"

"I. . . . I. . . ah. Well, you see Sara. I . . . uh."

Sara reached over and took his hand in hers, then said. "Samuel, just tell me."

So, he just blurted it out. "Sara, I'm just kind of like a ruffian of sorts. I'm not a gentleman of well being, but, my mind seems to think only of you most of the time. I'd be very proud if we could wed."

The statement was heard by Timothy and Susan as well as Sara. They all looked at Sara to see her response. A huge smile covered her face as she reached out and took Sam's head in her hands, lifted his chin up and gently placed a kiss on his lips. "Samuel Bowman, It would please me greatly to wed you."

She could see tears forming in his eyes, so she kissed him again. The room was quiet for several seconds as they all were beginning to understand what was about to take place in their lives.

Before the evening came to an end, the twins took them on a tour of the cottage. They started upstairs first. There were four apartments upstairs. Each one consisted of a bedroom, a bathroom a sitting room and a dressing room. Each also had a fireplace as well. Sara's was at the back corner of the house and Susan's was in the opposite corner of the house at the front over the wrap around porch. Downstairs they were shown the mud room with the maids quarters off of it, then the large kitchen, the pantry, the then dinning room where they had, had their meal then to the library, and finally back to the Parlor. When Sam and Tim were at the front door ready to leave, Sara once again kissed Sam. His heart soared with delight.

THIRTY EIGHT ✭
NEW CHESSMEN

During the first few days that the new chess pieces were being used by the ongoing group of visiting chess players everyone from the carving room would occasionally and casually glance into the chess clubs playing room to see if they could hear any words being spoken about the new chess pieces. Samuel, himself, who normally looked after this part of the club tried hard to overhear any conversation in regards to the new chess pieces. As it happens, the random chess club players who had been using the new style of chessmen designed by Jesselyn, had accepted them readily. A few had mentioned them briefly, but that was the end of it. Sam was excited because he knew that In fact these new chess pieces would have a lowered cost of making them. And would make the chess sets much more available to the common man. He would also find that sales would soar as these new chessmen were discovered.

With this kind of reception and acknowledgment of a different kind of chess piece, that was going to become the only kind used for the visiting chess players.

THIRTY NINE ✷
THE QUEEN'S CHESS SET
Sam had found some elephant Ivory available, though it cost
a tidy sum, he had purchased it from a man who had been in
Africa, though he was himself a 'Portuguese sailor.' A man
he thought to be from Portugal. A man who also said he
could get more if it was wanted. Sam knew it was African
Ivory so he had agreed to purchase nearly any amount if it
was good Ivory. He explained he'd had no use for poor grade
Ivory and he let this be known as well. He'd begun to carve
the minor pieces first, but would wait to make the King and
Queen until he had chosen the best Ivory for their places in
the chess set. The Pawns could wait as well as they could be
fashioned for smaller pieces of Ivory that would not lend
itself to the carving of the Minor pieces.

For the chess board he had decided to use a very limited
supply of African Padauk, a very rich red color, and Ardu,
from India which was a very pale yellow, but much closer to
white. The outer edges of the chessboard were going to be
from a dark walnut. The squares would be of Buffalo horn for
the black squares, and Ivory for the white squares.

He would use his best knives, saws and chisels daily until the
set was finished. Often his work was interrupted by a chess
player who came into the shop and wanted a game. He would
start a game with them, and if another chess player came in,
Sam would beg off the game to let the new arrival a chance to
play as well. Then he could return to his artful carving of

chess men. He expected the cost of the white pieces and the white squares to come to one hundred pounds sterling.

The Queen's chess set when finished would be over three hundred pounds sterling by itself. When this chess set was finished, and delivered with the chess sets for the Royal families children the Cheque from her Royal Highness would be enormous . At least to his way of thinking.

FORTY ★
JOHN'S VISIT

It had been one of the few of John's trips home, and he had come by the shop each time, but this time when he had entered the chess shop it was very apparent to everyone that the time he was spending in the Queen's court with the royal family's ongoing chess lessons, that the changes in Johns attire and vocabulary had been changing. He no longer wore the clothing of a youngster who would be found gallivanting about the towne's wharves. John was learning manners and words that had much more meaning than he had used in the past. Words that could have come from beyond the area where he had been raised. It wasn't an unpleasant change and his attitude toward those while in the company of the shop had not wavered. John was becoming, . . . polished. He had asked Sam for, and been given one of the new chess sets as his own that he could take back to the royal household with him. One he could study his games before he offered them to others. Also, he had started keeping a journal of his games and his way of doing things when he taught others how to play, or better their game of chess.

While he was there he and Sam played a game of chess. One of the few that they had played in quite awhile. While Sam watched John make his chess moves he became aware that John seldom made a move that did not contain some degree of a threat. This was of interest to Sam because he realized that those who played against John were, in a sense playing a continuous game of defensive chess.

Had he not noticed this about John's game, he too might have acted defensively. Instead, he attacked John's position. Then he watched as John had to stop and think more deeply about his next move as well.

FORTY ONE ✭
THE SQUARE
Samuel and Timothy had intended on going to their bank to
add to their account, but they had arrived too early and the
bank was not yet open. So, they ventured onward, ending up
in the Towne square. They had stopped just inside the square
and Samuel said. "It has been some time since I passed this
way, Tim."

"Aye, myself as well."

As they hesitated there, an ice van stopped in front of them.
No doubt on its way to the row houses and their ice boxes not
far beyond. It had stopped to wait for a hand cart that was
moving past on its way to the towne's open market. As it
moved on Samuel pointed out a wet spot on the cobble
stones. "Tim, have a look. You see where the ice melt
dripped on the stones. How much darker they are than the
others around them?"

Tim had noticed the change in color but paid no heed to it.
He started to move on, but Sam caught his coat sleeve and
said. "Lets move to the middle of the square." They moved
slowly looking at the walls of buildings, many with balconies
as well and that it was the buildings, that formed the Square.
When the two men reached the center, Sam stopped. Timothy
watched Sam as he seemed to be checking the cobbles at their
very feet. Then Sam's head lifted slightly and he began to
examine other stones around them.

"Tim. If you look around you will see that a master mason placed these stones in place."

"You know this how?"

"Look at the stones you are standing on carefully. You'll see a pattern. Then a different pattern of stoned next to them. And beyond that the same pattern you are on is repeated. Every other group of stones are the same as the two groups we are on."

Tim looked and he saw Sam was correct. "And we need to know this why?"

Samuel had seen some children playing stick ball on one side of the square. "Tim, hold your spot for a bit."

Timothy watched as Samuel went to the children. He could see him talking to them and then he pointed a finger at Tim. Presently three of the children came his side. They said nothing, so he asked. "What is it he's up to lads?"

The youngster looked up at Tim and said. "I don't know, Sir. But he promised a silver penny for standing in different places in the Square. That's a fortune sir. A bloody fortune you ask me."

Sam walked with one of the boy as he counted stone patterns. Finally as he looked to where Tim was with the other three boys, he stopped. He pointed his fingers at the lads next to Tim, and one of them ran to Sam's side. He left the first boy where they had been standing, and took the newer boy with him. Again he started counting stone patterns. He stopped again at a new spot, and left the boy there. He then pointed to another boy by Tim's side, and that lad went to Sam. This time he cut across between Tim and the first boy, until he was at what Tim now realized, was a square within the square. He left the third boy there and called out to Tim. "Tim, if you will Join me."

When the two men were in the center of the square that the standing boys formed. He said. "What you see Tim. Is sixty four squares of stone patterns. A chess board if you will."

"Well now that we know this, you have to realize that the stones are all the same color. Sam."

"Aye. That's so, when they are dry. But not if some are wet."

The trip to the bank had been forgotten about. Sam gave the boys the silver pennies he'd promised and the two men returned to the shop as they discussed the towne square.

FORTY TWO ✶
MATILDA

Sam had taken Sara with him to the bank a few days back. He'd spoken with the new accounts manager, Mister Hightower about his thoughts as to holding a chess tournament in the towne square and how it could come about, and it could be done if they had the well wishes from the Towne's Councilmen. He had received a non-commitment from the man, but he seemed interested an had said he would make inquiries on Sam's behalf.

This wet rainy morning as he and Tim were having tea at a playing table in the shop's chess room, they heard the tinkle of the bell up over the door, and as they looked to the door, a young attractive woman had come inside. Her umbrella dripping water on the floor, but she paid little heed to its doing so. Instead she spoke directly to the two men, and said. "I'm Matilda Owens. I'm to speak to Mister Bowman."

Sam raised his hand. "I'm Samuel Bowman. You look chilled, why don't you put your umbrella in the stand by the door, and leave your rap on the coat hanger as well. Then, if you like I'll fix you a cup of tea."

She was taking her coat off as the smile widened across her face. "I would enjoy that Mister Bowman. Thank you."

Sam acquired a clean cup from a shelf behind the chess display counter while Tim moved another chair to the table they had been sitting at. He held it for her as she sat. Sam had gone to the heating stove at the other side of the room and fixed her a cup of tea from the tea kettle that was on top of the stove, keeping the water hot.

As he placed it in front of her, as he asked. "Matilda, you say you have something to say to me?"

She finished taking a sip of tea and began. "I'm Mister Hightower's assistant and he asked me to convey to you that he would like your company at ten of the morning, next Thursday. He's arranged for you to speak to the Towne's Councilmen in their chambers."

Sam replied. "Tim and I will indeed join him for that purpose."

She looked quickly around the room, then said. "I've heard talk of your shop, Mister Bowman."

Sam and Tim both looked at her, the question not yet asked. When she continued. "All good has been said about the two of you."

Sam asked. "Do you play chess Matilda?"

"No. But I know of the game, Mister Bowman."

"Matilda, My name is Sam, if you please. And, if you've an interest in learning the game, It would be my pleasure to teach you how to play."

"I've not much interest in the game, Sam." She smiled as she used his name and avoided the more social rule.

"You know, Matilda several Gentlemen from around towne come here to play chess. Many are married, but a few are well to do bachelors."

Her cup of tea stopped just short of her lips as she grasped his meaning. "'Do They now?"

"Yes, usually on Wednesdays and Thursdays. Early evenings as it were." .

"Do many women play chess, Sam?"

"Many women play chess, but not here. Including the Queen. But I believe you would be readily accepted to the group. You would be an unusual player here I suppose, but, a challenge never the less. "

Now she had placed her cup gently on the table. "How long will it take to teach me how to play?"

He smiled as he said. "A life time."

"Surely you jest?"

"I can show you how the pieces move in less than an hour, but once you start playing chess you will find it is a continuous challenge to become better at the game, so the learning goes on as if there is not end to what knowledge you can gain."

"When do we start?"

"At your convenience, Matilda."

"Will others know you are teaching me the game?"

"If you prefer that no one knows of your interest. I can teach you in our carving room. Only those who work here will see you."

"Very well. I'll let you know when I can do this."

As Matilda left the shop the rain had stopped and her world had just taken a turn for the better, but she would not realize this for some time in the not to distant future.

FORTY THREE ✭
THE COUNCIL

Anthony Hightower had accompanied Samuel to the council meeting and had introduced him to its members upon arrival. The two men then sat in chairs that were there for the public should anyone care to observe the committee while in session and while the councils members dealt with the current matters at hand. When these matters were finished, one of them asked. "Mister Bownan I'm to understand you have a proposal for us?"

Sam stood and began his spiel. "Gentlemen you may not be aware of the fact, but the cobble stones in the Towne square are a thing of beauty. They are very well arranged. Meaningful in patterns of . Five stones in one square area and then six stones in the square next to it. Those patterns is then repeated on and on, one after the other."

One of the councilmen raised his hand and asked. "Is this an important matter Mister Bowman?"

"It is indeed if you wish to hold a chess tournament for the Townes people in your name. Something that will bring about a favorable remembrance in your honor as leaders of the people, sir."

This caught the attention of all of the councilmen. It would be a good thing to bring about a promising feeling toward them. Most often what they proposed raised opposition to them.

Another councilman then raised his hand and asked. How would this. . . this tournament take place Mister Bowman?"

Sam then went into a more detailed explanation of what he had found and how it could be used as a large chessboard. How he thought one pattern of stones could be painted with chimney soot mixed with water like a paint, and that it would wash away with the next storm. That and the other patterns could be left as they were. Also that he could bring the chess pieces needed for the games, and that he would expect two members of the council to attend the festivities and that they could also bring a guest to be one of the chess players during the games.

The seven men of the council gathered closely by themselves for several minutes while Sam and Mister Hightower waited quietly. Then just as quickly they returned to their seats and the man who was heading the meeting spoke up. "Mister Bowman. We have decided to accept your offer. If we can help in some manner, please contact any one of us for our assistance."

"Thank you. I'll begin with arranging the items I need and will keep you informed."

FORTY FOUR
THE SEAMAN'S REST ✳

Late morning as Sam entered the failing building, he came across the old woman who was the Inn keeper of the establishment. She had seen him before and remembered that he had at one time been a man of the sea himself. "Elp, you, Sir?"

Sam came right to the point. "I'm in need of a ship's carpenter. One in need of some work for a spell, but not as long as a voyage. Is there one here abouts that you know of, Madam?"

She searched her mind and came up with. "There be a youngun. Says he's had some experience in the yards and he's been a lookin. Don't think he's found nothin yet, though. And, he's owin me a few pounds. You wait here and I'll be fetching him for ya."

The young fella was a bit rough looking. Sam figured he'd been out of work for a spell and now he needed a shave and a bath. Sam motioned him outside so they could talk without being overheard. Then, "The old bat said something about you might have a chore or two for me, sir?"

Sam wanted to know if the man was to be counted on. "I'm Samuel Bowman, and you are?"

"Harvey, sir. Harvey Stengould."

As Sam reached into his pocket for his money purse, he said. "Harvey, here's two pounds. You get yourself cleaned up and shaved, then come to the back door of the chess shop. It's just past 'The Queen's Inn" And, I'll tell you what it is that I'm in need of."

Harvey was greatly surprised. This man did not know him, yet he was giving him two pounds to start with. "Thank you sir, Thank you. When do you want me there?"

"The sooner you get there the sooner you'll find work with, and for me."

Harvey had nearly run to the bathhouse. Then he's shed his whiskers and put on clean clothes. Nervously he knocked at the back door to the shop and a lovely woman opened it for him. "Ah, you must be Harvey. Sam said you would be by soon. Come in. Come in. I'll fetch Sam."

When Harvey entered the carving room, he couldn't believe his eyes. There were two of these wondrous creatures. Sam took him out to the playing room to explain what it was he wanted. Fortunately Harvey knew what chess pieces were. He' never played the game, but he had seen chess sets along the way in his life.

Sam explained that he wanted Harvey to find the wood, cheap if possible, and to carve eight Pawns and they were to be knee high. He wanted four knights and four Bishops and they were to be mid thigh high.

The two Kings and Queens were to be as high as the waist. It could be any wood as they would be painted black and white when they were finished. They should be of a size that would allow them to sit on their base and not fall over. But that they could be moved without much of a struggle. If he had any questions as to how the pieces were to look, he could ask Sara, or Sam himself.

FORTY FIVE ✫
MATILDA & THE EARL
It was to be Matilda's first game in the clubs playing room that it had happened. It was early evening and it had been quiet during the day. One or two players had come and gone and Sam was going over an opening move with Matilda. The bell over the door tinkled as the two of them spoke and as Sam looked up and over Matilda's shoulder he saw a man he had not seen in some time. As he neared the table where the game was set up he said. "Mister Bowman, so good to see you again."

Sam did not want to scare Matilda so he replied. "Mister Hamilton. Welcome sir."

As Matilda looked up, the gentleman noticed the beauty of her and asked. "Miss, do you mind if I draw up a chair to observe your game?"

She looked quickly to Sam, and he nodded his approval. She then said. "If you please. Yes."

"Mister Hamilton, this is Matilda Owens. She's new to the game and could use someone other than myself to help her improve her game abilities. Would you be interested in helping her along this path by chance?"

Matilda was about ready to get up from the table and to escape from a confrontation to her game ability, but as it happens, the two men sensed her discomfort and the Earl said.

"My lady, it would pleasure me greatly to attend to a woman of beauty such as yourself and her needs in learning the game of chess. If you would permit me to do so. . . . Please."

And so it happened. Sam excused himself after a few moments and he was not missed. The Earl was taken with Matilda, and she with him. It would cause a ripple of excitement through her later to find out she had been playing chess with The Earl Hamilton.

FORTY SIX   ✲
HARVEY

Harvey had come across what he thought of as a treasure.
He'd been to the shipyard looking for something he could use
to carve the large chessmen out of, when the yard master
found him wandering around the yard and did not know of
him.

"You've business here. Sir?"

Harvey just took a chance and said. "Sir. I'm in need of wood
to make into chess pieces for Mister Bowman and the chess
club. He's the man who's to make the chess pieces that are to
be used in the Towne square chess games. This be part of
some Towne council's doin."

The yard master knew of the man's name mentioned. He'd
shared a glass of Ale with him in the past. "And what kind of
wood would you be needing?"

"Something light in weight would be best, and I'll be needing
near sixty feet of wood."

The yard master took a few moments to search his mind.
Then he said. "Follow me." He led Harvey down to a lower
part of the yard, and it was cluttered with various ships
debris. When he stopped, he pointed at a long ships mast.
"This is a cedar mast that had dry rot at the bottom and had to
be replaced. It's be yours if you want it.

I'd like to get it off the yard, and can offer you a helping hand to haul it away. In fact I can also let you have a wagon to do so as well."

It took Harvey two days to cut the mast into pieces he could use, and another day to load and haul them to the porch on the back of the chess clubs door. He and Samuel were pleased with what he had done in such a short time.

Harvey read his list again so he could plan ahead to what he had to do..
Pawns to be to the knee high.
Minor pieces mid thigh high.
King and Queen to be waist high..

He had stacked the rounds of mast wood on the back porch of the shop and was given a corner inside the shop for his work area. In the beginning he was noisy, but this would fade as he made progress. Still he tried to keep it quiet. Not muttering to himself seemed to help. At least he thought so.

He started by using a small ax to cut away most of the center area and the rounding of the top of his first Pawn. The work had gone slowly at first. There was a great deal of wood to be removed from the round pieces of ship's mast to begin looking like something that Sara would approve of. He had asked Sara for her opinion as he did so on several occasions. And, with her guidance the work progressed fairly well. Sam had said little as Harvey used his ax and heavy chisels and rasps to fashion each piece. It was Sara he had to satisfy and she was a tough taskmaster. Once he had come into his own rhythm, things were going much better.

It took him the whole first day to make his first Pawn, and it still needed to be smoothed like that of the skin of an apple. He thought about his progress as he headed back to the "Sailor's Rest" for the night. At this pace it would take him over a month just to make the Pawns. He envisioned a sea serpent whose tail went on forever.

As it happened the Pawns took a day each. The Rooks were eight days each. The Knights took another ten days each. The Bishops, seven days each. The Queens eleven days each and the
Kings came to twelve days each. Before he was to finish them it would take him one hundred and forty two days to make the set of chessmen to fill Sam's needs.

In the end he would use nearly every bit of the mast wood that he had for the chess pieces and the chips he would cut away would be used in the heating stove to heat hot water for tea for the folks in the carving room.

FORTY SEVEN ✶
CHESSMEN FOR THE SQUARE
It had been late morning when Sam came near the growing
pile of wood chips and was looking at one of Harvey's first
Bishops, and Harvey ventured a thought. "Samuel, I've
looked at your chess tables in the playing room and I've an
idea. I can inlay chess squares into the tops of the tables.
Then you would only have to let players use chess pieces and
not chess boards as well." The picture came to Sam's mind as
he asked. "You are meaning that you can place colored
squares into the chess tables wooden tops?"

"Aye, that's my thinking. The idea came to me when I saw
the box of chessboard squares Sara told me you wouldn't use
for your chess boards because they weren't good enough. I
think they will do well for the tops of your chess tables."

"Harvey, you're a man of many abilities and talents. I may
have to keep you employed for some time. But, yes please do
inlay some of those squares into the tops of our tables and
we'll have a look at them."

The Bishops were now being carved, but the Pawns had been
finished. The Rooks would come next, then the Knights and
finally the Kings and Queens. In the end it would only require
that the painting of all of them as to their playing colors
would be the last thing to do before the tournament took
place in the late following spring.

FORTY EIGHT ✶
CHESS IN THE SQUARE

The thought of a large chess set and used in the public square
had come into Sam's mind months before. Now it was about
to take place for the first time, and if the towne council found
it popular they might agree to the use of it once or twice a
year. Doing so, would be good for the chess shop and, the
council as well.

The chimney sweeps had come through with the chimney
soot which they had made into a paste and placed it onto the
squares at Sam's direction. He had large ships water casks
along the edges to protect the chessboard from treading feet.
He had also hired the same older boys who had stood at the
corners in the beginning. They were to help control people
who were watching the games taking place. He would also
use the two older boys to move the chess pieces as needed at
his and Tim's direction.

Two large dray wagons were used to transport the chess
pieces to the square in the early morning hours, that and
sixteen chairs to be used by Sam and Tim and the dignitaries
that would be included in the chess games in the square. This
would be one councilman, his choice of who would play
chess against another councilman across on the other side of
the chess board and his chosen guest. Both in different
wagons. Sam and Sara were seated in one wagon and Tim
and Susan in the other wagon on the other side of the chess
game.

Just before the games were to begin Sam saw the Earl with Matilda on his arm in the crowd and went to them. "Sir Hamilton, why don't you and your lady join us on the viewing wagon just there." He pointed and the Earl responded. Mister Bowman, we would be delighted to join your group."

The councilman, and his guest were surprised and happily made room for the Earl and Matilda when they took seats on the wagon. It appeared to them that Samuel has many influential friends.

Fliers had been distributed throughout the crowd to let them know the rules. The games were to last no longer than one chime of the Towne's tower clock. Decisions, if needed will be made by the master chess player, Mister Harwick as the judge.

A toss of a coin revealed that the councilman with Timothy and his guest friend, had the option of playing the white pieces. The older boys' Samuel had hired, and been under Sam's tutelage for the past few weeks, were waiting just below his wagon and he spoke quietly to them. They moved quickly to place the chess pieces in their proper squares with the white pieces below the wagon opposite his just outside the roped off area of the chessboard. .When the pieces were in place, the two boys, one wearing a white shirt, the other one wearing a black shirt, stood by the wagon who was to play the chess pieces of their shirt colors.

It had only been a few minutes before the tower clock chimed the hours time. It seemed it was only a few seconds before Timothy leaned over the side of his wagon and gave his lad the instructions as to which piece to move.

In Samuels wagon, the councilman's friend was faced with the first move of his opponent. It had also written down on a record book by Sam.

1.d4 After a moment of his own, the following move had been made and recorded. d5.
After the next few moves were made, and Sam looked at his notes, then back at the chessboard below his wagon, he was surprised that the player in his wagon had made a surprise forking move that left him with a good center position.

1.e4, e5
2.Nf3 Nc6
3.Bb5 Nf6
4.0-0 Bc5

Sam called out softly to the councilman's guest. "Sir. Consider using your Knight to capture the King's Pawn on e5."

The man looked, then over his shoulder he replied. He'll capture my Knight with his Knight on c6."

"Yes. He will, but you can then move your Queen's Pawn to d4, which will fork his Knight and Bishop. You will end up with equal material trades and have a good center position with a threatening Pawn. Also as he can't save them both, whichever one he saves will tell you which piece he treasures the most and you work on getting those pieces away from him. Thus weakening his game ability."

He turned to look back at Sam, smiling as he said. "Mister Bowman I must come by your chess club and discuss my chess future, if any." Then he turned back to the game and made the move Sam had mentioned. It seemed to Sam that there was two conversations taking place between Tim and the councilman in his wagon, were they discussing the game, or was it something else that was distracting the two men. Still it was only a short time before Tim's group had tipped the King as it were. Signifying their loss of the game.

As the following games took place during the day, the crown had thinned out with only the most enthusiastic chess players from the surrounding neighborhoods in attendance. As each game was played each time with the councilmen's new guests , the groups of kibitzers from the sidelines of the game were heard to groan and moan as their choice of players played the game and as blunders were made and that were costly to that player. The chess games in the square were the topic of conversations for weeks to come. Many who knew of the game began to take an entirely new interest in playing the game of chess.

FORTY NINE ★
TIMOTHY

Two days later Sam and Tim were sitting at one of the chess tables with the new inlay work that Harvey had done. "Sam, I've something on my mind that I need to tell you about."

Sam put his tea cup down. There was a look on Tim's face that looked serious. "What is it, Tim?"

Tim looked around the room, as if to see if anyone else was about. "At the square, and during the chess games, The councilman, in my wagon told me in confidence that he is soon going to be leaving the area. Which will leave a vacancy on the Towne council and I think he took a liking to me and Susan because he asked if I would be interested in taking his place on the council."

"And, you told him what?"

"He told me this after we talked about my knowledge of the waterfront. I told him that as a seaman I spent a great deal of time along the waterfront. And that I would discuss his offer with you and those that matter in my life. Then I would tell him of my decision"

"Timothy, my friend. You would do well to accept the position if it is offered to you. However, . . . there is one more thing that you should consider doing as well, and it is a matter of great importance.."

126

Tim sat up straighter in his chair and looked at Sam questioningly. "What, pray tell would that be?"

"Don't you ever tell anyone I told you this, but, Susan asked me why you have not asked for her hand in marriage ?"

"She asked you that? Holy yardarm, Sam. I have never dreamed of such a lovely woman in my life. Do you think I should do that?"

"If you care for her in that way, I think you would be a fool not to do that. Especially a man of your means and with a possible position on the Towne council as well."

"And what of our business here at the club?"

"It seems as though most of our business now concerns our chess sets, and I think we are going to start using Harvey to make some quality chess tables as well. In time you and I will be stepping aside and we'll have to let someone else run this place for us. At the moment we have barely have enough hands to fill our orders for more chess sets. I get more orders for chess sets and chess tables in the Post every day, so We'll be needing to find a few new apprentices. Especially after Sara and I are wed. Even you and Susan, if that should come about. The two of them will be wanting to raise a family which means they will be staying home, and not spending time here in the carving room."

"Sam, I knew when those two came in our door the first time, that our lives would never be the same again."

"Tim, I'm also of a mind to teach John how to get things done here. So, that at some time he can take over the shop as well."

"You know, Sam. The chess shop has done well. But, my part concerning the 'Scrimshaw' has not brought in much of the monies for the shop. Not like I would have hoped anyway. Yet you continue to share the monies from the chess club with all of us. That's a good side of you. That's another reason I'm thinking of dropping my anchor in the Towne's council if they will have me.. There's a wage there and I'm warming to the idea of doing that kind of thing in my life."

"And, Susan, Tim?"

He smiled broadly as he said. "I'll pull Susan alongside to raft up with me, Sam."

FIFTY ★
JOHN'S VISIT
John had spent every day of his home time this time, at the chess club. At a slow time of day, on one of those days he and Sam were sitting at one of the tables with the new inlaid squares, and John said. "Sam, I've been asked if I would like to go with the Royal family to their summer Manor house with them for the summer months."

Sam looked to the lad's eyes, and he wasn't sure, but they seemed, . . . sad in a way. "Your Mum knows about this does she?"

"Yes. We have talked about it and it is okay with her."

"So, are you going with them then?"

"I'd rather stay here at home and to come here each day instead."

"Then that's what you should do. We'd like to have you with us as well." A huge smile crossed John's face and he got up from the table. "I'll go tell Mum that I'm staying here then. I"m thanking you Sam."

"No need to thank me, John. You're like one of my own, you are. And while you are here then, it's time you learned how to run the playing room as well."

FIFTY ONE ✶
JOHN
LESSONS
A thought came to Sam's mind as he looked at young John.
He'd met the lad when he was but seven or eight at most.
Now he figured that John must be ten and four. Maybe more.
This thinking came to him when John had asked for Sam's
permission to offer chess lessons here at the club, and that
idea had been quickly accepted by Sam. "Of course, John.
But, you should charge a fee for your giving them the
knowledge of how to play proper chess."

Once the word was out about the lessons being taught they
had both been surprised at the amount of those wanting to
learn from John. There didn't seem to be many who wanted
Sam to teach them, it was John they wanted to have teaching
them the finer points of the game. John had an understanding
with those he took a students of the game. They could not tell
others what they were paying John for their lessons. To do so
would bring about the end of their lessons with him.
Many regular patrons of the club just wanting to become
better players were among his students.

One of those who came in was an additional surprise. As it
happens, it was Matilda. She was quite good at the game but
had an agenda in mind.. The Earl had introduced her to the
Royal family and Matilda wanted to be able to win her games
in that high circle of acquaintances. With John's knowledge
of the Royal families chess habits, their game weaknesses and

strengths, he was able to guide her in ways that would often give her an advantage.

Late one afternoon, while John and Sam were waiting for William Harwick to come into the shop. John said. "Sam, there's a chess game I'd like to bring into the shop. I'd call it the 'Port and Starboard' chess game."

"I've not heard of that game before. How does it play?"

"I'd have Harvey make the new chessboard, and it needs one hundred and sixty squares. That, and two complete chess sets of chess pieces will be used. It has four players divided into teams of two each. And, they play against one another until both Kings of one team are check mated. They cannot speak to each other about the game before them while it is in play without a penalty."

"How is it you know of this game?"

"I had time in the evenings while not teaching chess to the Royal family, that I would spend in the largest library in the whole of the Kingdom. Mister Thorton, The Queens Envoy, made me aware of the chess books they have. I read about this game while there. It came about in the fifth century, but it was quite different then. Still I think it would be welcome here."

"John, that would be as sight to see. Even to watch such a game in play would be something that might gather a crowd of kibitzers. Let's give it a try."

The bell over the door tinkled as William Harwick entered the shop. He spied John, and asked. "Would the teacher of the Royal family have time for a game?"

Sam left the two of them seated at a central table and at times he went to the table to see how the game was progressing. Each time the two players were quiet, no words were being spoken, their eyes locked on the game before them. It was as if there was a tension in the air around them. When he had looked just now from his seat behind his counter, he saw William reach across the table and offer his hand to John. Sam's eyes widened at the sight of what he had just seen. He believed that William had just congratulated John for winning their game.

He watched after William left the shop without further word, John was making notes in his journal about the game. Sam knew the journal held much more than chess notations. It was a history of Johns and his world of chess. That, and how he thought the game should be played.

FIFTY TWO ✷
THE STREET HUSTLER

It was midweek and one of the few days that Sam cane to the chess club. He was sitting at his usual table. John was presently at a table reviewing a chess game that two players were at odds over who had the better chess position before retiring the game.

Sam was listening to the banter as John pointed out the difference in game strengths and weak points between the two sides of the chess board when the bell over the door tinkled it's melodious tune. When Sam looked that way he was surprised to see a very young lad standing inside and looking lost. Sam said. "Can I help you lad?"

The youngster looked his way as he said. "Aye, sir. I'm in need of a chess set, I am."

"Come sit here lad." Sam had pointed to a chair at his table. It was easy for Sam to understand this was someone not used to any of the finer things in life. This child's clothing was that of a street urchin. A child who spent most of his day begging for anything he could get.

The youngster came over and struggled some, but was able to pull the chair out a bit so he could climb up on it. Finally he was settled and looked at Sam expectantly. "I'm Sam and who might you be?"

He sat up straighter now. The old man speaking to him seemed gentle like and had not told him to be gone. And he had given him his first name and not the name of Mister something. So, he would be polite like his ma had told him to be. "I'm Jeremy, sir."

"So, Jeremy. You know the game of chess do you?"

"I know how the pieces move, sir."

Sam almost laughed at the comment the boy had made. How many times had he heard that over the years. "Sit a spell I'll get a chess set and you can show me what you know about the game."

When Sam came back he had one of the chess sets that those who came to play would have paid a fee to use. He also had two sweet rolls as well. He put the bag of chess pieces on the table, then said. "Jeremy, I've come across two sweet rolls. If you've no objection perhaps you could eat one while I eat the other one?"

A sweet roll was something Jeremy had never had before, but it looked good and it was food. "Aye, Mister Sam. I can do that." The sweet rolls had a very short life span as they were quickly devoured. Sam's lasted a bite or two longer, and when the two of them had finished them they both licked their fingers and wiped them on their trouser legs.

Sam emptied the chess pieces out of the bag and said. "Jeremy, set up the chess board for us now."

As he set them up Sam asked. "How is it you know how to play chess Jeremy?"

"Mister Perkins showed me how to play." He tilted his head a bit as he was thinking. "I think I was five or so. But he's passed on now and his brother took the chess set home with him. So I've not played in a spell."

This did surprise Sam. "And lad, how old are you now?"

"I'm nearing seven now, mister Sam" Jeremy had set the board up properly, and Sam said. "You play white, Jeremy."

Thankee sir." And he moved the Queen's Bishop Pawn out two squares. Sam responded by moving the King's Pawn by moving it out two squares.

By the time they had both made their seventh move, Jeremy's game was in trouble. Sam said. "Jeremy, you know lad that chess sets are not cheap toys."

"Aye, sir, I watched the chess games in the square and knowed I could come here to ask for a chess set, sir. If I had a chess set, I could set it up someplace in the towne square and play chess for a silver penny, or two."

Sam had to smile at this. As he thought about this young lad as a chess hustler in the square, he knew that Jeremy would likely do well at this kind of thing. He was polite, but his mind was working constantly. He had a quick tongue when it came to making others seem comfortable with him in their company. That and he was honest about what he wanted to do with the chess set.

"Does your Mum, know where you are and what you are wanting to do with a chess set?"

"Me Mum's a washer woman. She gets up with the sun and works until it goes down. She lets me fend for me self, sir."

This came as no surprise to Sam. "Jeremy, lets take a walk to the shop next door. I want you to meet a fellow over there that might be able to help you come by a chess set."

"That would be a blessing sir." Sam took him in the back door of the carving shop and led him to Harvey's own table he used for his records and the like. Harvey saw them coming and stood, but with eyes that were questioning what was going on.

Sam said. "Harvey, this is Jeremy. He's in need of a chess set. I was thinking he might be of help to you in some way as to work a trade. As we have chess pieces that the new carvers had done as they learned to carve, but that we cannot use to market, perhaps . . . "

136

Harvey knew where Sam was going with this comment, so he said. "Jeremy, would you have the time to come here three days a week and sweep the floors for me?"

Jeremy was quick to understand he was being offered a position. And that, that would help him get a chess set. "Aye, Sir. I can do that easy, sir"

"You are to start tomorrow then?"

"I can be here early, sir"

"Come with me then."

Harvey took Jeremy to a box where the rejected chess pieces were kept and told him to choose the ones he wanted. That and a chess board that had also been rejected for one reason or another. While Jeremy was going through the chess pieces, Harvey came back to Sam. "How long should we use him to make the chess set of some value to him?"

"As long as you, and Jeremy are comfortable with each other and you are satisfied he has earned the chess set you are giving him."

"Sam, you know those chess sets are of little value."

"Not to him, Harvey. To him they are like gold."

*　　　*　　　*

It was several days later when Samuel had gone to the bank to speak with Anthony about his accounts. Then after he left the bank he decided to take a stroll around the towne square just to see what was taking place. As he arrived at the last corner of the square on the far side, he caught a glimpse of the street urchin, Jeremy. He had his chess set perched upon an upside down ships water barrel. He was just starting a game with a man whose clothing showed him to be above average in well being. Samuel moved closer so he could watch the game in play. It lasted a mere seven moves. Jeremy had played the 'Scholar's Mate"

After the game was over there was another man waiting a turn at the chess board against a mere child. Sam spoke to the one he had watched playing the game with Jeremy and asked. "So, is the boy any good at the game of chess?"

"That he is. I left three shillings with him."

Sam just had to get into this, and he said. "The next time you play chess with him, make him a higher wager to make him nervous and you should play slower."

"You play chess do you?"

138

Sam smiled as he said. "Well, I know how the pieces move."

As he turned to head back to the chess club he thought. *"Well, I think I've just added a few more shillings to Jeremy's purse."*

He knew that playing chess slower against Jeremy would not make any difference at all.

Days later Harvey tells Sam about Jeremy's sweet talking the women of the carving shop, and how they were taken by him. To the extent that they might get him a winter coat.

FIFTY THREE
WEDDING PLANS & ✳
NUPTIALS LIST
It had taken weeks of planning, but the wedding was finally
scheduled. Beforehand Sam and Tim had been introduced by
the banker, Mister Hightower to a tailor who's shop was one
of those around the towne square. The tailor knew he was
going to have his hands full. He found that these two men of
the sea who had no idea of how to dress properly. It would
fall on him to delicately give them the information they
required for such an important occasion. Yet, he felt in doing
so they would become long term customers.

For Sara and Susan it was not going to be a hindrance in any
manner. They had been raised in this kind of social circle.
Still, they would explain things to their soon to be husbands
as the time drew near. They both understood they would have
to save the two men from some social embarrassments that
could come about.

The wedding was to be a small quiet affair, and they had
arranged for the Vicar to preform the ceremony in their home
at the cottage. The immediate guest list was short as it
contained only the names of their close and current personal
relationships. The housekeeper that had been in service to the
family had not, as yet, been found. The twins had fond
memories of her as children and wanted to include her if they
could find her. Also, the neighbors who lived just next to
them would be invited. After some hesitation and discussion

it was decided to add one more name to the list. A name that would cause some lively entertainment among their guests. A man so different from their normal lives that Susan and Sara giggled at the thought. A man that their men were well acquainted with. A man who was a trader in goods, so to speak. Shandy's name had been mentioned by Timothy, but it had not yet made the list. Still they envisioned a festive occasion and to be enjoyed by all.

Sara looked over the list one last time. Then handed it to Susan for her opinion. It read.

Earl Hamilton
Matilda Owens
Richard Humphry
Anthony Hightower
Captain James Neuman
Jesselyn & John
Harvey Stengould
Martin
William Harwick
Shandy & friend

The two women smiled as they talked about the mixed group that would be attending the wedding. Even with the limited amount of those attending, it would be a mixed lot. Sailors, and the well to do gentry sharing this occasion together would be entertaining in itself..

FIFTY FOUR
STAUNTON & COOK ✻

It was common for chess players to be waiting outside the shop's door as they waited for Sam to unlatch the bolt each day. Today Sam noticed a gentleman just outside the door who had himself waited until the others were inside, then he too, entered the shop. Sam was waiting for him near the door as he had not seen this gentleman before. When he came in, Sam extended his hand in welcome and it was taken.

"Welcome, Sir. Are you here for a game, or can I offer you something else, sir?"

"You must be Mister Bowman. I was given your name at "The Queen's Inn. My name is Cook. Nathaniel Cook. And yes if you've the time perhaps we could indulge ourselves in a game while we speak, sir."

"I'm beg your pardon, sir. But, I'm just opening the shop and need to finish my work first, but, why don't you sit at one of the tables. I'm sure it won't be long before someone else comes to play a game of two."

Sam led him to a nearby table that he had already set up with one of their newest chess sets. The pieces were of Jesselyn's new design and with more detailed pieces. A chess set that is in itself a simple beauty of intricate carving and of rich hardwoods. The table was also one of the newest tables with the inlaid chess board imbedded in its surface.

The bell over the door tinkled just at that moment, and another young gentleman entered the shop. Sam approached him and bid him good morning, as he usually did those who came to play chess. "A good morning to you sir."

"And to you as well, sir. I've just arrived on the packet ship, and we are to be moored here overnight before my voyage is to continue. I spoke to the Captain about something to fill my time while we wait for the high morning tide on the morrow. He mentioned your chess club. As a chess player I thought how wonderful, a few games to pass the waiting time with a pleasure across the chessboard."

"As it happens good sir. Another chess player is waiting for a game as well."

Sam led him to the table where the first gentleman was studying the chess pieces while he waited. "Mister Cook, this is. . . "

Sam turned to look at the latest gentleman, perplexed that he had not gained his name. Whereupon he, himself held out his hand to the fellow at the table. "Staunton, sir."

As he stood to take his hand, he replied. "Mister Staunton, I'm Nathaniel Cook. It would be my honor sir to have a game or two with you, sir."

Again the bell over the door tinkled with it's melodious tunes. It was Vincent coming inside. He spent many days in the chess club and was known by many of those who frequented the club. Without hesitation he made his way right to Sam's personal table. Sam came alongside and greeted him."Vincent, a good morning to you, sir"

"Good morning Sam."

As he sat, Sam said. "Can I get you some tea, Vincent?"

"That would be an accepted kindness of you Sam. Please, if you will."

The stove had, had a fire burning long enough to heat water for tea so it was only a minute or so before Sam returned to the table. "The King's tea is yours when you like, Vincent."

Vincent understood what Sam had just told him. He meant that his cup of tea was on the King's side of the chess board. Sam did this to letting him know where his tea was to be found, and at the same time not letting anyone who was new to the chess club know right away that Vincent was blind. As Sam turned away he noticed the two men he had just introduced to one another, were actually fondling the new style of chess pieces. Admiring their beauty and to them, unusual design.

In moments Sam had returned with Vincent's traveling chess set. As Vincent checked each chess piece and placed the chess set in his favored space on the table, Sam left him to finish opening the shop for the day. Still, he kept an eye on the two new men who had come to play chess. He had observed that after observing the board for some time, Mister Staunton played the Queen's Gambit and Mister Cook played the French opening. He over heard Mister Cook remark.

"The opening move is sometimes difficult, is it not, sir?"

"I find it so. At that point I simply do not have any idea what is going on."

Later, after Mister Staunton had left the chess club, Mister Cook came to Sam and inquired, "I would like to have one of these new style of chess sets, if you have one available, sit?"

In moments Sam had the new, and quite detailed and expensive chess sets in a nice chess box ready for him. At the closing of the sale, Mister cook said. "I thank you Mister Bowman. This is the reason I came by your shop." And with that he bid Sam a goodby, and left the building.

FIFTY FIVE
WEDDING   *

The invitations had been hand delivered, and each one
happily accepted. So, on this Saturday morning the four of
them stood facing the Vicar in the parlor as he read the
wedding vows to each couple. After the vows had been taken,
the four of them greeted their guests and bottles of fine wine
were consumed. Several empty bottles of wine were
discarded in the kitchen trash bin.

Sam had been watching Shandy and his friend, Lizzie as they
mixed among those who the two of them felt were well above
their station in life. He could see the two of them had dressed
in their finest Sunday clothes, and it was passable as social
attire. Not that it mattered to him. Lizzie was one of the
women who served Ale and chips to those who frequented
'The Queen's Inn' However, what really surprised him was
how Sara and Susan had taken Lizzie under their wings, so to
speak. Lizzie, as it turned out had a boisterous laughter when
something humorous was revealed to her. A laughter that was
infectious and enjoyed by all who heard her.

On one of the few times that Sara tore herself away from the
other groups to speak to her newly wedded husband, she said.
"Sam, did you know Elizabeth was at one time a member of
the Royal house keeping staff?"

"You mean, her name is not Lizzie?"

"No, silly." She smiled, then continued. "It seems as though she spoke her mind to the head housekeeper one day, concerning a matter that Elizabeth thought to be wrong. The head housekeeper sent her packing. Out the door never to return."

"So, that's how she came to be at 'The queen's Inn?"

"Yes. So, Susan and I have made an offer to her. I would like you to go fetch her and her things on the morrow, and bring her and her things to our housekeeper room off the mud room and kitchen. If you will?"

Sam understood the reasoning behind this request. There would now be more work to keeping the house in order with the four of them living here. A house keeper would be an added bonus. "Consider it done my sweet."

As the day wore on their guests reluctantly found their way out of the cottage and returned to their own lives. None had wanted to leave the festivities.

Time just seemed to disappear and finally Sara took Sam's hand and led him to her bedroom. In moments Tim and Susan found their way to Susan's rooms as well. It seemed a quiet night, but that was only because the conversations were now more hushed whispers than anything else.

The following morning as the four of them sat at the kitchen table finishing their breakfast, Sam said. "Sara, you are a most delightful woman."

"I'm glad you enjoyed the taste of me Sam."

Susan only smiled at what was being said. Tim had no idea.

Late morning Tim and Sam were heading for the chess club. The two of them knew they had to move their personal belongings to the twin's cottage as that was to be where the four of them would maintain their residence.

FIFTY SIX
ELIZABETH ✶

Her day had started out way beyond her normal self. Shandy had come to her two days before and asked if she would like to attend a social affair, and a wedding, as it were. At first she thought he was making it up to get her to bed. Then she began to realize he was truthful in his question. Now, today, and after Mister Bowman had come with a carriage and all, to fetch her to his home, she was almost overjoyed with happiness. As she was putting her meager belongings away in her own private room, and Armoire, a knock at her door. She moved to the door, and upon opening it she found Sara waiting to speak to her.

"Elizabeth. On the morrow Susan and I will take you to a shop in the square to obtain new clothing for your position here, if that is not offensive to you?"

"Oh lordy, missus Bowman. That would be wonderful, thank you so very much."

"Elizabeth, my name is Sara."

"Yes, mum."

FIFTY SEVEN ★
HARVEY & JESSELYN

Samuel and Timothy spent most of the day removing their belongings out of the apartments up over the shop to their new home. The twins cottage. The two of them had not known of a previous discussion that had taken place between Harvey and Jesselyn. But, that would be revealed soon enough.

Just before Sam left the shop with the last of the smaller items, Harvey approached him, saying. "Sam, if you have a moment. I've a question."

"Aye, Harvey. I've no need to rush now."

Harvey quickly looked around, as if someone might overhear what it was he had to say. "Sam, as you know, the apartments upstairs are now empty. Could I use one of them for myself?"

Sam knew Harvey was still keeping a room at the 'Sailor's Rest' "I see no reason why you should not do so. You will have to keep it tidy of course, but yes go ahead and move your things into either apartment."

Now Sam noticed that Harvey seemed even more reluctant to continue the conversation, but after a few seconds he asked. "And if Jesselyn wanted to use the other apartment for her and John. Would that be okay as well?"

This did surprise Sam. He would have to tell Sara, but the answer rested with him. He did not ask why Jesselyn needed a new place of residence, he simply said. "Of course she can use the other apartment as well."

Later, as he and Sara were in their rooms at the cottage he had told her of the new tenants above the carving room shop. She had added. "They will be carrying some 'Ballast', but it should not be a part of our personal business."

FIFTY EIGHT
THE MAIL PACKET SHIP ✶

Harvey and Jesselyn had both asked for three days away from the shop. The reasons for doing so were unknown to the others at the time, but the time away had been met with approval. Sam, Sara and Susan knew they could manage things well enough. They were far enough ahead in tables and turnings that the two of them would not be missed for this short period time.

It was late afternoon when Sam and John were setting up a chess game to play between themselves that Sam learned of what was taking place with Harvey and Jesselyn while they were away.

"So, John with your mum gone for a few days are you fixing your own meals?"

"That I am. My mum was very pleased that Harvey asked her to go a voyage on the packet ship to wed."

Sam sat up much straighter, very surprised as he said. " I don't understand what it is you have just passed along to me, John."

John smiled broadly as he explained. "They took passage on the mail packet ship. It takes three days to make its way up channel, then to return here. The Captain said he would wed them at sea and that it would be a legal marriage."

Sam enjoyed what he was hearing, but asked. "Are you okay with this John?"

"Yes, sir I am. Harvey is good to me, and he is very good to my mum."

"I'm pleased with this, John."

"So am I, Sam."

As the custom had been taking place since the four of them were living in the twin's cottage, they adjoined to the parlor after dinner. Here they would discuss the days events and latest gossip from around the towne.

Sam led it off with. "I'm to understand that Jesselyn and Harvey are going to be wed on the packet ship as it sails up channel, and before its return here to Port."

Sara, Susan and Timothy were stunned and silent for several moments. Then the barrage of questions started. Finally all Sam could do was say. "I have no more knowledge than what I've already told you. We will just have to wait and see what they tell us on their return.?

FIFTY NINE
THE BRAGGART *

In the recent few days a man had been coming into play chess. He had not been well accepted to begin with as he was not shy about letting those in the playing room know how good he was at the game. Part of the problem was that he was good at the game. But should have just kept his mouth shut about his ability. He had confused a few players with his glib tongue and he had talked them into wagers which he won handily. Sam wanted to get rid of him and his obnoxious ways but could not come up with a solution. Until this morning.

When Mister Braggart 'That's what they called him behind his back' came in, Sam confronted him right away. "Sir, I don't believe you are as good at this game as you would have us believe."

"Mister Bowman. You show me someone you think can beat me at this game and I'll wager you any sum you like,"

Sam tried to keep a smile off his face as he said.. "On the morrow I'll just open the door and ask the first person that comes by to do the honors of playing chess against you."

He could hardly believe what he'd heard. That would indeed be easy money. "Why wait until then?"

"Because there will be many of those who come here that will want to watch the game in play."

"So, be it then."

Sam had been busy the rest of the day yesterday making arrangements for the game to take place today. When Mister Braggart arrived he was met by a room nearly full of chess players. Some of whom he had taken a pound here and there from them over a game of chess. He only smiled as he sat at a table that seemed to be waiting for two players. "Well then, lets get on with it."

Sam asked. "You mentioned a wager before. I'm wondering if you are still of that thinking today and before the game starts?"

"Of course. But let me see who's to play."

Sam, turned to John who was waiting close by. "John, why don't you open our door and reach out to whoever passes by and get that person to come inside to play a game of chess with this gentleman."

John nodded his head as he moved to the door. He opened the door and everyone waited for someone to pass by. When it happened John quickly reached out and said.

"Please, if you will, join us for a few minutes."

As she entered the shop, she seemed reluctant to do so. There were a good many men here, she the only woman. "Please, my lady. If you will sit here and let me tell you what it is we are in need of." He pulled out the chair opposite the Braggart, and she sat demurely.

When she sat, she looked down at the table and said. "Oh, you're playing checkers I see."

"Well, not exactly. It's a game called 'Chess' Are you aware of the game?"

"Oh yes. I've heard it mentioned at the salon. It seems to be a game that men play at."

"Would you mind if John here shows you how the chessmen move, and then perhaps you could play this gentleman a game to test your skills?"

"Surely you jest, Sir?"

"Well it is said that chess is above a woman's skills, so if you would rather not play. We'll understand."

The woman seemed to bristle at the fact of what had been said. So. "I think I would like to give it a try."

Sam pointed to John, "My lady, this is John. He will tell you how to play the basic game of chess."

As young John came to her side, she said. :John, my name is Matilda."

"Yes mum. I'm John."

While John was explaining the way the chessmen moved, the braggart stood up and moved by Sam's side. "About that wager, Mister Bowman. What did you have in mind?"

"Make it easy on yourself, sir"

"Would twenty pounds be too much for you?"

Even Sam was surprised at the amount proposed as a wager.

"I think those in the room who would be watching can come up with twenty pounds if need be. So, yes, If you can do the same give it to John to hold while the game is underway. I'll do the same."

Braggart offered his hands with a Pawn in each of them to Matilda. John said. "Matilda you can choose this hand," he pointed at the left hand, "or this hand." And he lightly touched the right hand.

John of course had counted the seconds in his head and knew where the white Pawn was being held. Matilda understood what he had done so she made the choice.

"Let me see." She began by moving her fingers pointing at each hand in succession. "Eeeny, Meeny, miney moe. Oh, I suppose it doesn't matter. I'll choose the left hand."

Braggart was perplexed as he opened the hand she had chosen and handed her the white Pawn.

Matilda picked up a Pawn and said. "Now I just put this infantry man down somewhere is that it?"

"No. On the first move you can move it one or two places straight ahead." Having said that, John had to smile. Matilda was a devil at t he chess board.

So Matilda's first move was the Queen's Pawn to the fourth square in front of the Queen herself.

Braggart did the same with his Queen's Pawn. Then Matilda moved the Queen's Knights Pawn out two spaces. Smiling, the Braggart quickly captured the Pawn with his King's Bishop, but was surprised when Matilda moved her Queen's Bishop Pawn out one square. This threaten his Bishop so he had to move his Bishop to safety, but only moved it to stand on his Queen's Rook four square. Out of play, as it were.

The game had been played many moves and had gotten down to Braggart only having his Queen, a castled King still in hiding and a Knight, Matilda had only her castled King, also on his castled position, a Rook, and a Queen's Knight Pawn still on its home square. She just moved her Bishop to a square where it looked at the Black King's Bishop's Pawn.

Braggart saw an opportunity and moved his Queen's to the Queen's Bishop's home square. He was pleased because now he had the white Bishop pinned in place. If the White Bishop was moved, he would capture the offending Rook on the other side of the board and checkmate the White King. Then he would claim the wager and be on his way. Accept, . . . he overlooked one small item. It was her turn to move. She had set up a trap for him. An oversight on his part as it were. Now she moved the Bishop and in doing so captured his King's Knight Pawn and said. "I think that is what you said is Check."

Braggart was angry with himself he had no option, he had to move the King out of check and in so doing he captured the offending White Bishop. And watched her Rook swoop down to capture his Queen. As he studied the board for the following few seconds he was aware his King was to far away to catch the now moving Knight's Pawn, and it would finally be promoted to a Queen and his game was over. He could not fight against a Queen and a Rook.

159

He simply got up from the table and left the chess club by the door she had used to come inside. As he walked down the road he said to himself. *"I'll never return to a place where a woman has taken a chess game from me."*

Later, Matilda would explain to the Earl, that she had used the 'Evan's Gambit opening.'

SIXTY
TIMOTHY
COUNCILMAN ✭

Tim had been taking several days away from the shop. The time he needed was expected as every one at the shop understood he was trying to get approval as a councilman for the towne. He had been fortunate in the sense that the district he was to represent was an area where he was well known. The district was the entire waterfront area where he had spent most of his time as a seaman. To include all of the wharf facilities, the warehouses, the shipyards and all of the shops that operated in the area. He had been spending time to visit every one of the businesses that would come under his influence as a councilman. He had been readily accepted and the word was out in his favor. In less than a fortnight he had been sworn into his new position.

Those in the shop would miss him when he left them, but they were pleased he had taken this turn in his life and was going to do well.

SIXTY ONE
JOHN ⋆
VINCENT'S LESSONS

It was mid morning when a woman came in the door, she
looked quickly around and in seeing Sam, asked. "My father
needs to rest a bit. Can he sit at one of your tables for a
spell?"

Sam, was quick to her side. "Surely he can. Where is he/"

"Just outside. I was on my way to the market and he had
asked to go with me just to get out of our dwelling for a spell.
But these days he tires easily."

"By all means lets get him inside."

The woman turned on her heels and just called out to the man
waiting on the porch. "Father, come in you can rest here."

Sam was surprised as the man searched about with his
walking stick as he took each step. Using his walking stick to
find his way inside. He was apparently blind, She led him to a
chair and as he sat he said, to whomever might be listening.
"I thank you sir."

Sam replied. "You are welcome, sir" Then he turned to her
and said to her. "Why don't you go about your shopping and
stop back by on your way home?"

"You're a good man, sir and I thank you for your courtesy to my father."

After she had gone Sam had gotten the two of them a cup of tea. Sam had given the man his name and learned he was speaking with Vincent. He watched as the older man was careful with his cup. Then he said to Sam. "What kind of shop is this, sir?"

"It's a chess club."

"Ahh. . . chess. Yes I remember when I was younger I played chess on occasion. But now. . . well you can see that I cannot see."

A thought crossed Sam's mind and he said. "Let me show you a chess set." He was only away from the table for a short time. When he sat back and sat down he put some chess pieces and a chess board on the table in front of him. "Have a look at this chess set."

The older man smiled, he was aware that the man near him knew he was blind, yet he was offering a chess set for him to look at. He put his cup down carefully and reached out with his fingers. When he found the chess pieces he felt each piece carefully and the chessboard as well. "The chess pieces feel beautiful, Sam. But I don't know which are the white pieces or the black pieces. Also, a chessboard with holes in the center of each square. Why is that?"

163

"It's a traveling chess set, but I'm thinking we can make a small change to the set so that you can tell the white pieces from the black ones. Then you could come here and play chess with the other members of the chess club."

The older man reached out to find Sam's hand and it was given to him. As he held it in his own old hands he said. "Can you really do that?"

"You come back on the morrow and I'll have a chess set for you to use when you visit us here." Sam new the chess set would seem odd to the regular chess players of the chess club, but not to the extent that it would change the game for them. It would however, offer a chess set Vincent could use, and it would be held for his use only. The black chess pieces would have the head of a very small nail protruding out of the top of each piece. And the black squares on the chessboard would be raised with a thin piece of dark wood that Harvey used for inlay work on the chess tables. With a hole now cut through the center of each so as to allow the chess pieces to be moved from one square to any other square like before.

This was to be the beginning of a relationship that would affect many lives over time. John was to take Vincent under his wing as well. The result came to the point, that there were chess players who waited a turn to play chess with a blind man. Not many would brag that they had lost a chess game to a blind man.

SIXTY TWO
BANKING ✮

While Sam sat across from Anthony this morning, and after
having made a deposit he had removed from his strong box at
the club, he had asked. "Anthony, the shop next to mine has
been empty for over a year now. I'm thinking of asking its
owner to let me purchase it, but I don't know who owns the
building. If I could get it for a fair price I could use it to move
our chess set carving part of the business into that shop
instead of in our back room where it is now."

Anthony smiled as he said. "Sam, the bank owns that
building next to you, and I'm quite sure it could be had very,
very cheaply."

Sam looked at him questioningly, "The bank owns it? And
why would it be let go for a small sum?"

"Because property in that area is not selling well. The banks
monies are residing there that could be more useful
elsewhere. At the moment the best investment in properties is
down on the waterfront. I believe that is why your friend,
Mister Rollins has taken options on two small shops on the
waterfront."

"Tim did this?"

"Yes, just this morning in fact."

Sam sat quietly for a few moments, finally he asked. "The shop next to mine, can I afford to purchase it?"

"Sam, do you heed any of the receipts we give you when you make deposits, or withdrawals?

Most often he would just stick these slips of paper in his pockets and eventually discard them entirely "Not really, why?"

"Sam, you are, in a sense, a wealthy man. You can easily afford to purchase the shop next to your present location."

That evening after dinner and as the four of them had retired to the parlor, the conversation about their daily lives were given for a family discussion. It was during the ongoing conversation that Tim explained the two shops he had purchased on the waterfront. It was the one he had purchased with the intention of giving it as a gift to Jesselyn for her use as a Madam's Coiffeur shop. Susan and Sara were aware of Jesselyn's past history, Sam was now informed of what had taken place earlier in her life. He was surprised that Jesselyn had been in service to several ladies of high standing. That she had, had an unusual ability to bring out the beauty of each of her ladies, and to make Jesselyn herself very desirable in those households.

Sara and Susan were of the opinion that she would do very well in her own shop. And Susan got up from her chair and moved next to Tim and kissed him. "More of that later my husband."

Sam did not know what they were going to do without Jesselyn in the shop.

SIXTY THREE
NEW LARGER SHOP *

The banker Anthony Thorton had seen to Sam's taking
ownership of the shop next door and he had asked Harvey to
take over changing it to fit their needs. After the two men
decided what was to be done, Sam left the chores to Harvey.
Then he went in search of Sara, Susan and Jesselyn.

Back in the carving room he gathered the three women
together, at the meeting table.

"Ladies. I want to move all of the carving benches, lathes and
work tables to the new shop next to us."

Susan asked. "What will you do with this room when we
move over to the new shop?"

"We'll use this place to keep the finished tables and chess
sets in stowage until we have someone who makes a
purchase."

Jesselyn asked. "Harvey told me that we are going to start
making boxes for our chess things so they can move by lorry,
or coach?"

"Yes, but we may have to find someone who can do that.
Which reminds me, we'll have to find some new helpers to
train to do the work you three are doing.

You are mot quite able keep up with the orders we are getting for our chess sets and tables."

Sara, ventured. "I've an idea where we can get some help?"

Sam looked at her, waiting for her to continue.

"I'll speak to Richard and ask him for a list of wives who's husbands are away at sea. Wives that are in need of some monies to help them feed their families, or even just for themselves."

"And, then what?"

"Then the three of us can see how well they do at carving, or turnings on the lathes. Once we find the best of them, we use their talents for the shop and its needs."

"When can this be done?"

"I can start this day, if you wish?"

Sam knew that this would indeed do good for the seamen's families. Perhaps even doing more good than the men's earnings themselves. "Let's get this started as soon as we can then. But something we should have the new carvers understand is that they cannot tell others what their wages are while they are with us. To do so will end their employment with us."

Jesselyn asked. "Why would we do that?"

"It will stop bad feelings between them as we will pay more to those who are showing us good workmanship and amount of chores they finish in time."

SIXTY FOUR ✯
NEW APPRENTICES

Sara had arranged for a delivered invitation to attend an afternoon tea at the new shop. It was a come-as-you-are gathering in one weeks time. Those who had children were welcome to bring the children with them, but that the children must behave. The note gave an indication of possible employment for those who might be interested. Nothing to indicate what was required for them to attend. She, and Susan had each signed the notes as well.

Shortly before the women were expected to arrive, Susan had arranged for the baker to bring sweet rolls and tea. The door had been left ajar so as to make it an easy decision to come inside. As they came into the shop either Susan, or Sara greeted them. Of the eleven invitations delivered, nine women attended, and not a child appeared. Though there were children at home being watched by an older sister, or brother, until their mother returned.

It began with introductions with Sara leading it off. She explained that she would point to each of then in turn and it was understood that, that person would stand and introduce herself to the others as well. After the introductions were finished Sara led them on a tour of the shop and explained what it is that they were doing here. She also paid close attention to the comments made by the ladies as each step of the carving procedure was gone over in some detail.

Susan took over from there and had them all sit down for tea and sweet rolls, as she explained what it was they would like to happen next. The women were interested should return home and come back in the following days to speak with, either her, or Sara. To discuss what part of the group they thought where they might be useful. This of course would not be the case if they were not interested in spending time here.

One of the women asked. "Do I understand there is to be a wage paid as well?"

"Yes. A starting wage will be given, and as you become better at what it is you have chosen to do, you will be given more in wages."

Another asked. "What will the starting wage be?"

A woman sitting near her said. "More than you're getting now. I imagine."

Susan liked that comment and made a mental note of who it was that had said it, but she said. "That's something we will go over with each one of you who start with us. That and the shop rules we have to put in place as well."

SIXTY FIVE
INTERVIEWS ✳

It had been a very busy morning as Sara and Susan each took turns interviewing the nine women who had returned to inquire about the tasks to be done in the shop. Each woman would spend some time with each of the twins in turn. It had been agreed that later they would discuss each woman and her potential, and what they thought she could do best.

They found that five of the nine were used to using a spinning wheel. And would be tried at the lathes. All of them made their own kindling for the fires in their ovens and cookstoves so cutting wood was a familiar activity. Still that didn't mean they would be any good at carving chess pieces..

All of them would be given a precut blank for the Knight with a finished sample to see how well they could copy one of those. They became aware that one or two of the nine struggled some at carving. But they could be of use with the turning lathes.

It was a surprise to the twins to find five of them were almost a natural at carving

Sharpening the carving knives was an easy test as they all were used to cutting their own meats at home. This too was a needed skill to do so properly.

The twins found that all of them seemed to get along well together. The social relationships came about along naturally during the time of day when rest periods and when tea was being served to them. Each woman had agreed to a schedule so as to take turns each day to make the tea for all of them to consume. Sara and Susan always joined in these tea breaks.

On one of the first mornings Sara gathered all of them around while they shared tea and biscuits form the baker just down the walk. "Ladies if you can come to an agreement as to the behavior of your children, you can bring them here with you. But they must be controlled as we do not want anyone to get hurt in any way. It is all up to you to work out."

During the days that followed the women worked out the details of how they could work with each other as to managing the children.

In time one of he women would be found to be careless, but Harvey found out she could make dovetail boxes quite well and she was also good at sewing the cloth bags for the chess pieces often used as well. This was welcome news to the twins. They simply did not want to let her go. Every one of the nine women were in need of these positions. Everyone feared the work shops for the poor and the debtor's prison. They were little more than slave labor shops.

SIXTY SIX ✶
VINCENT & THE EARL

On the day before the new women's group's long term training was to begin, Sam became aware of someone waiting outside the chess club's door waiting to get inside to play chess with someone. Though it was not yet time to open the door, Sam did so anyway as it was Vincent. There was no need to leave him out there so he opened the door and bade Vincent to come inside.

"Vincent, come in sir. Come in." As he kept his eyes on Vincent as he made his way to Sam's table, the bell over the door chimed again. Sam hadn't closed the door as he had wanted to be sure Vincent was seated at the table okay before doing so.

As Sam turned to see who it was that came in, he had to smile. "Mister Hamilton, good to see you sir."

The Earl knew Sam wouldn't use his Royal title in the shop as Sam was afraid the Earl would not get a fair game of chess. They both knew that his title of 'Earl' would often cause the other player to let the Earl win as a favor to him. An indebtedness as it were.

"Sam. Good to see you again." The Earl saw Vincent sitting at Sam's table and asked as he pointed at Vincent. "Do you think I could get a game in today?"

Sam had to smile at the thought of what may be coming about. "I think so Mister Hamilton."

"Vincent, this is Mister Edward Hamilton. He's interested in a game of chess. Do you have the time?"

Vincent knew that Sam knew that he had come in to play chess so he didn't know what to make of the question. "Of course. A game would be most enjoyable. Please sir, sit with me, sir. And Sam would you be so kind as to bring my chess set to us for a game?"

Small talk took place as Sam placed the chess set that he had made for Vincent down in front of him. The two men had already assumed a more personal relationship and were on a first names basis. Vincent reached out and plucked a white and a black pawn from the chessboard. He placed them behind his back and when his hands came back in front of him he held them out so Edward could choose one or the other. As it was, Edward had chosen the hand with the white pawn.

Before the game began, Vincent asked. "If you will, Edward. Tell me each time the pieces you are moving and the square to which it is being moved?"

It was a strange request, but it was not a bother. "Surely sir."

"One more request, please. Forgive an old man and let us forgive the touch move rule. If you touch a piece, you do not have to move it if you do not wish to do so. And of course you will forgive my sins for doing the same."

The Earl knew that nearly every chess player has some sort of oddity about them and their game as well, he simply went along with the request. "As you wish Vincent."

Just after his first move he said. "e4." And Vincent replied. Ahh, yes. Pawn to the Queen's four square."

Edward thought*"Of course. Anyone can see that was the move being made."*

Vincent's hand came out and after brushing over the top of the King's Rook and Bishop, he picked up the King's knight and moved it out into the game. He said as he did so. "Nf6"

More as a mimic, Edward said. "Yes, the King's Knight to stand in front of the King's Bishop's Pawn square."

After a move or two more, the Earl said. "This is an unusual chess set sir. The dark squares have an extra layer of dark wood, and the black pieces have a knob of sorts on top of each of them. That and the chess pieces each have a peg on the bottom, and each square has a hole in it."

"Yes. It is a travel chess set. Ship's Captains are fond of these chess sets as they keep the pieces in place when the ship rolls with the waves. But now this one may be the only one of its kind? Sam made it for my personal use only."

It was when Vincent's walking stick, that had been resting against the table, fell to the floor and he began to search for it at his side with his hands searching in vain before he finally found it and returned it to the edge of the table, that the Earl came to understand that he was playing chess with a blind man.

Then he watched amazed as Vincent looked at the chess pieces with his finger to bring into focus where each chess piece was currently in place so that he could determine his next move. The Earl became so engrossed in the ability of Vincent's game of chess that the two of them finally agreed to a drawn game.

SIXTY SEVEN ✶
JESSELYN'S TRAINING SESSIONS

There were five women attending that Jesselyn started training first to make Pawns on the turning lathe. Four of them did well, but one seemed to lack the feel for using a turning lathe to make round objects from wood. She was however, to become one of those that had a good feel for handling a knife when it came to doing the final intricate carving of the Rooks and Knights.

Jesselyn tried to make sure each woman understood what it was she was learning and doing, and doing it well. Jesselyn was concerned about taking her leave of the chess shop without knowing that her part of doing things was in capable hands. This feeling was because she had another adventure waiting for her and she wanted to get it started. She would miss the daily banter of the shop, but a future had been offered to her and she did not want to miss the opportunity.

SIXTY EIGHT ✶
MADAM'S COIFFEUR

When Harvey was satisfied with the ability of the new
women working for the chess club, he had asked for and was
given permission to let Jesselyn take time away to try get her
ladies' shop open on the waterfront. If it came about as a
success, she could take her leave from the shop and with the
good wishes from everyone.

Her first day in her shop was busy with her arranging the
items needed to take care of each lady who might come her
way. One woman who had just been walking by did stop in
and was pleased to see such a shop being opened. While there
she made appointments for her and her two daughters the
following week. That was how it started and it was but a
short time when the word was out about who she Jesselyn
was, and that of her history in the higher social circles in the
past. Within two months time her shop 'MADAM'S
COIFFEUR' was among the waterfront shops most
successful. From walk in ladies to those with fancy carriages
were found arriving often during the day.

She had two other young women in her employee withing the
following weeks. Daisy was the youngest and Lizzie who was
older, just happened to look down into Jesselyn's private box
on the cabinet behind her station in the shop.

Each of them had a similar box so as to keep the extra monies they night receive that clients might leave her for a job well done. Lizzie hadn't meant to be nosy, she had just come to ask a question about doing a certain hair style.

She couldn't contain her curiosity though when she had looked down. What she saw was round with a shiny surface and resting on a velvet bag. This took place just as Jesselyn looked up at her at the same time.

Her hand came up to her mouth in amazement as she said. "Jess, what is that? It looks like a man's . . . . "

"That's what it's supposed to look like, Lizzie." Jesselyn looked around quickly to be sure Daisy had already left, then she continued. "Often our ladies who come to us to do their hair or make up supplies are wed to men who are away at sea. Sometimes for months, or even years on end. This is something that helps them get through those times when they are in need."

Lizzie asked. "Is this something I can tell someone about?"

"No. Not openly. However, if it is a person you know well and can trust not to say where it came from, we can obtain one of two if we have a friend who needs one. Still, you must know they are expensive." Jesselyn knew very well that Lizzie would be selling these toys often. She didn't reveal the fact that it was she herself that spent a few hours in the evenings at the turning lathe. Then with the use of good carving knives, some smoothing paper and a few coats of good varnish, she could produce any kind of pleasure toy a woman might fancy.

The shop was so busy it became necessary to make appointments well ahead of time. And often a conversation taking place between Lizzie and her charge was about being able to comfort one's self with a husband gone for a spell.

SIXTY NINE
SAM & FAMILY ✶

Many months after the wedding, Sara, on one evening while she and Sam were lying quietly in bed said. "Sam. The chess club and carving shop are doing quite well, are they not?"

"Yes my love, they are doing very well indeed."

"Perhaps, then you could spend more time here at home with me, and our children?"

Sam turned and raised up on his side leaning on his elbow, his hand reached for her breast as he said. "Sara I can do that, but we have no children."

"But, we are going to have children, Sam. The first is only a few months away."

He kissed her on the lips, thanked her for being his wife, then they made love again.

SEVENTY ★
JOHN

Sam knew John was able to easily run the chess club, but he put the question to him one day during a chess game. The game was more of a lesson for Samuel, as usual, but still a welcome event and time he could spend with John.

"John, would you be interested in taking the helm of the chess club for me?"

John's hand stopped in mid air, a Pawn awaiting its final destination. "Do you mean to be the shopkeeper of the chess club?"

"Exactly that John. It would of course include a wage higher than you are getting at the time. But one I think we can come to an agreement on."

"And what of you, Sam. What are you to be doing?"

"Well, I will come in from time to time, probably often, but Sara tells me I'm to be a father and that she would like me to be home to help her with our children when they arrive."

John smiled as he thought of Sam becoming a father. He had certainly been good to him in all the time he had known him. And now John had a 'Pa' in Harvey as well. "I'll make sure to make you proud Sam. I can run the Chess club easily."

The next day, John had moved Sam's table to a position more suited to his liking. As of now it would be known that it was 'John's' table to those that frequented the chess club. Sam had just smiled when he first saw what had taken place. *"No matter."* he thought.

SEVENTY ONE ★
HARVEY

A few days later, and after speaking with all the others working in the carving shop, Samuel had Harvey join him for a pint at 'The Queen's Inn' They had settled at a corner table well away from the others who spent many an hour here. Sam asked. "Harvey, Johns taking the helm of the chess club as I won't be there every day now."

Harvey stopped with his glass halfway to his lips and said. "Aye. John has told me about his new position. That's good of you Sam."

"Well, I'd like you to take the helm of the carving shop, if you will?"

Now Harvey had a wide smile on his face. "Sam, I would be proud to do so."

Sam smiled as he said. "Well, you would have to accept a larger wage as well."

In Harvey's mind he was thinking. *"Jesselyn and I are going to be wealthy."* I can use the monies as well Sam."

SEVENTY TWO
JOHN'S JOURNAL ✫

One of the chess club's members business was unknown to those who frequented the playing room. One day after a game between John and himself, and as he was pulling his coat off the pegs by the door, he saw John making notes in his journal. Without speaking, at first, he moved over to the table once again. What he saw was a thick booklet of hand written notes and with a few chess notations on the top sheet.

"John is that a record of your chess games?"

John was well aware that many had seen him making notes in his journal over time. "Yes, Mister Steed. It's memories' of chess games and my thoughts about chess. Things about chess that I have been keeping for a few years. I have seen many games lost that could have been won, and games won that could have easily been lost. I've been writing my thoughts on how chess should be played."

"Could I have a look at your journal for a few moments?"

John could see no harm in that, so he said. "Sit yourself sir, and have a look. I will enjoy your opinion on my notes."

It only took the turning of a few pages, before Michael Steed looked up at John and said. "John, do you know what my business is?"

"No sir. I do not."

"I have a printing shop, John. I make books. And I think you should make this into a book for others to read and to purchase for their own libraries."

"Do your think others would purchase a book like this?"

"Of course they would. And, you my young friend could make a good deal of money from its printing as well."

SEVENTY THREE ✶
AT HOME

The children were in bed and fast asleep While the four of them were sitting in the parlor long after dinner sharing a bottle of good wine. The discussion was about times past. That and the young woman John had met recently when she came into the chess club. Her family had just arrived here recently, and new to the area. She had been surprised to learn of the chess club and decided to pay a visit. They smiled as it was revealed that John t it upon himself to fix her a cup of tea while she sat at his own chess table. The one that Sam had kept for himself in the past.

Sara said. "Apparently the two of them had gotten along quite well, and John had remarked repeatedly to Sara while she had been there, as to the young woman's qualities. Sara knew that this was a relationship that would flourish if given a chance.

Tim brought up a subject that Sam had as yet to hear about. "Sam, the council members have decided that the chess games in the Towne square should become a yearly event." Sam had to smile. "I agree with them, Tim. I still hear talk among others about the games as they took place when we put them on display the recent past. Sir Hamilton was equally impressed. He mentioned that he would like to see the Queen have an chess board built into the castle's courtyard so visiting members of the Royal family could experience an open chess game for all to watch, and that they could participate in themselves.

Late in the night, with the wick of the lamp turned down low, it gave an air of warmth to the bedroom. Sam and Sara were lying in bed talking about their lives and how things had taken place. As they began to grow sleepy, Sara said. "Sam, kiss me before we sleep."

She felt Sam's hands reaching for her. Sleep would not come just yet.

EPILOG & HISTORY

Samuel Bowman

Samuel was orphaned as a young lad when his parents were taken from him by the black death. By chance he had entered the offices of 'Humphry Shipping' one cold winter day just to warm himself by the wood heating stove. Richard Humphry discovered him there quite by accident. Partly because his secretary, Martin, hadn't shooed the boy away and had taken pity on the poor lad. Richard had shared some crackers and cheese, along with a hot mug of tea to warm the boy as they talked. In the end Samuel was taken aboard one of the ships owned by Richard and taught the "Ropes" which he quickly learned was how to adjust each sail and the like. Eventually he became a ship's Boatswain. One of the ship's carpenters on a ship taught him how carve and made him carving knives and then gave him part of a whale tooth to work with, or so he remembered. As it happened, one of the first mates taught him how to play chess. It was on a piece of sailcloth with squares of dyed colors and the pieces were pebbles and sea shells of various kinds. One thing led to another and he became a carver of chess pieces. When in home waters and ashore, he played chess at "The Queen's Inn."

He had a special sea chest of his own and one that is hard to open as it has a lid that is held in place by a combination a locking mechanism of sliding wooden parts.

This sea chest was made for him by a Chinese craftsman who made it like a Chinese puzzle box. The chest was heavy from the weight of his tools and supplies.

Timothy Rollins
As a youngster, Timothy was also taken in by Richard Humphry and put aboard a ship as a cabin boy to begin with, finally to become a boatswain like Samuel. In that position he met Samuel and the two men had become friends. His father had been a farmer who often sold vegetables to the captains of ships moored to the docks. Somewhere along the way he found his time off watch was spent learning how to carve symbols and figurines on fish teeth. Actually the tusks of walrus's. And he became a well known Scrimshander. As it happens he ends up becoming a member of the Towne council. His district will be the waterfront and all of the businesses.

Cabin boy - John
This was Johns first voyage, and he's apprenticed to the captain, and he will become a fountain of information to those he favors. As it happens John is very good with numbers. Unbeknownst to most, John is the son of Jesselyn, the mistress of Reginald Bowers. The ships pilot who was also to become a chart maker. During the time John had first signed aboard 'The John T. Franklin' he became friends with the Bosun, Samuel Bowman, who taught him how to play chess, he started keeping a journal so he could remember things he had learned.

This habit continued for several years until finally a printer friend, of the other Bosun, Timothy Rollins who had become a Towne councilman, and who had known about Johns journal and had mentioned it to a friend of his, a Mister Steed, who upon reviewing the journal offered to print it in the form of a chess book. "How not to play the game of Chesse." It went through three printings and made John a tidy sum. As it happens a few of those who had purchased John's book came by the chess club to have him sign their copy. His service to the Queen's family as a chess tutor was, in a sense, short, he had changed a bit. Nearly becoming known as a gentleman as well.

Richard Humphry
Had become the owner of the shipping company - "Humphry LTD" through an inheritance from his father, who in turn had inherited it from his father as well.

His secretary - Martin
Was always old, or so everyone thought. At one time he'd been asked if he wanted to retire with a small pension, but he'd declined. He needed something to do with his time.

Ships Captain
Mister James Neuman - Ships master for thirty-four years. He'd started as a mate on one of Richards fathers ships. The "Celeste". He had proven himself capable of handling authority and had been given command of a small mail carrier ship used by the Royal family. Now he was captain of the larger vessels owned by the company.

Mister Mirelles
Mirelles had served on several ships over the years, but upon learning that the 'Humphry Shipping company was good to those in their employ. They paid in wages or shares of the cargo when sold. He was a First mate for them for seven years as first mate. He may have a future as a ship's captain.

Mister Mason
Mason had a similar history and also signed on with Humphry shipping some five years ago as a second mate. He may eventually become a first mate, but probably not much more.

Mister Shandy
Shandy is one of those characters that are found roaming the dock in search of making a fast shilling when he can. Samuel and Timothy take advantage of Shandy's skills so he finds Ivory and Walrus tusks for the shop. He also comes across Stag and Reindeer horns as well.

He buys with funds provided from the shop and collects a small fee from the seller. Usually a few silver pennies for his effort on their behalf. He ends up with a regular group of ship's carpenters who bring him all kinds of exotic wood and whale bones as well.

Ships carpenter
He was never known by any other name. But he was a dedicated crew member for Humphry Shipping. Because of this he was allowed to stay aboard the ship even if it was in port. Like a permanent fixture. This worked out well as he maintained many things while spending his days aboard.

Sara & Susan - Twins
The twins are introduced to Samuel and Timothy as apprentices in the new chess shop. They are a part of Richard Humphry's family relations. Their own parents died when Cholera spread throughout the area while they were younger and Richard took over looking out for their well being. He has continued in this endeavor, but then he saw the potential of Samuel Bowman and Timothy Rollins.

Jesselyn
Jesselyn, Johns' mother had been in service to the wealthy ladies of the Towne. She had a reputation of being an absolute artist when it came to a woman's need's to look her best at social functions. Then she had met the chart maker, Reginald Bowers, who had an apartment up over his shop that she could use as her own dwelling in which to live.

When Timothy had arranged for her to open her shop "The Ladies Coiffure" on the waterfront she had done quite well. Also she seemed to have access to ladies toys when they asked for them. They were accepted gratefully and were well made and carved to perfection with a very fine varnish finish on them. In the long run of things she becomes a well established shop keeper herself. This after many other un-expected changes in her life.

Ships carpenter
Harvey Stengould. Who will carve the chess pieces of the towne square chess games. And reveals he has a talent for doing inlay work as well. Samuel was thinking that perhaps he could even make chess boards for the business. Then Harvey and Jesselyn become involved with one another. In time perhaps moving into the apartments up over the shop when Sam and Tim wed the twins. In the end Harvey was to become the overseer for the carving shop. They would have nine women who had become good at the task given them for carving chess pieces, Two would find an ability to do inlay work as well.

Ships blacksmith
Smokey was one of those who always seemed to show up as the company was selecting ship's crews for a voyage somewhere. Where he went when the ship was in its home port, no one knew. He just waited around to get paid off, then he would disappear. Some figured he had family in a distant village.

Ships sailmaker
Needles worked part time for a shipyard, but enjoyed time at sea. So, when a Humphry ship was going somewhere, he signed aboard as crew. He knew the trade well and was found able to repair most any torn sail. Or, if he had the supplies he could make a new sail. There were times he had a lot of deck space covered in sail cloth while at sea.

William Harwick
William of Surrey, was how he was known. A chess master it seemed. He'd started out as a lad going to a free school in his towne. As it happens, the head school master took an interest in him. It seemed he had a good mind, he was just not interested in learning. One day the head master was about to scold him for causing a ruckus in class, but he noticed that William was fingering his chess set. He was a man of some means and had acquired the chess set from his friend the towne Bishop, as it were. Without thinking he'd begun to explain how the pieces moved, and William asked questions that were meaningful as to the game. That had started the relationship that was to blossom into Williams playing chess against others who would challenge the head master to a game. He became unbeatable. In time his reputation grew to the extent he was invited to chess clubs in many places. Often far removed from his home. He was to take John on as a chess student and had done well in his teaching.

Howard Staunton
Though Staunton was not the original designer of the Staunton style chess sets used even today, this style was named after him, and continues to be known as the 'Staunton Pattern.' I've no knowledge of who actually came up with this style, nor am I aware of anyone else who knows of its origin. But it came into use in the 1800s.It was introduced to Staunton by Nathaniel Cook.

Reginald Thorton
The Queen's envoy who came looking for "John, the chess player."

Anthony Hightower the banker, and man who help further the lives of what were initially, men of the sea.

Matilda Owens
Hightower's assistant. And who was to become a favorite with the Royal family after she learns to play chess and meets the Earl. In time she will become a more prominent member of the Royal family.

Sir Edward Hamilton
The Earl, plays chess at the chess club, but without most knowing his Royal title. In time he will wed a Royal family favorite.

Mister Steed
To become the printer if Johns journal on how not to play chess.

Port & Starboard Chess
This is actually a chess game that came from centuries ago. It is a game that requires four players. Commonly known today as "Partnership chess."

Jeremy
The street chess hustling Urchin

Ships name - John T. Franklin
Ship square rigged - Spanker, two working jibs, one topsails on the mainsail mast, wheel helm, covered binnacle, large hold for cargo of spices. Crew of 56 Length of 118 feet. Holds 740 tons of cargo

Cargo
Pepper, Cloves, Cinnamon, Mace, Nutmeg, Wines.

Ship's articles
Punishments included being "put in irons" and flogging (whipping). If a man disobeyed orders or otherwise displeased captain or mate, he suffered one or the other. The "cat-o'-nine-tails" (a whip of nine knotted lines) was often used. It was painful for the crewman who experienced it, and frightening for others to watch.

The chess Queen
Queen Theadorah of Byzantine, Catherine, the Tzarina of all
Russia, Queen Isabella of Spain and Queen Elizabeth the first
of England, were all accomplished chess players and held
sway as to the strength of today's chess Queen and her ability
in the game of chess. The Queen we use today did not exist
as such, before these Queens influence into the manner of
play.

Other books by Donald L. Boone

Chess Stories Through The Ages
Chess Tales Of Kings And Queens
Mastering Basic Chess
The Chess Set
The Chess Game
The Scholastic Chess Coach
Those Who Play Chess
Mister Bones & The Scrimshander
Chess Histories And Mysteries
Chess Records